TAATA

Time And After Time Ahead

By Robert Joseph Coleman

Time And After Time Ahead: TAATA

A Meredith *Etc* Book
Meredith *Etc*
1052 Maria Court
Jackson, Mississippi 39204-5151
www.meredithetc.com
2nd Printing
Copyright © January 21, 2020 Robert Joseph Coleman
96 pages

Foreword by Meredith Coleman McGee

Published simultaneously in softcover/hardback
Hardback 6"x 9" printed by Barnes and Noble Press
Black and White on White paper
ISBN-13: 978-1-734578-1-9
Trade paperback 6"x 9" printed by Kindle Publishing
Black and White on White paper
ISBN-13: 978-1-7341578-2-6
106 pages
21,817 words
1st printing
Copyright © 2001 Robert Joseph Coleman
Art Concept 2001 Jozzlyn Janika Coleman
Published by BCII Publication - CM Coleman, CFO
Library of Congress 2001-130669
ISBN: 0-971-3374-0-3

Made in the United States of America

DEDICATION

Robert Joseph Coleman II (1961-1989) &
Ronald Barry (1962-2019); sons of the author.

ACKNOWLEDGMENTS

The author is pleased to thank Almighty God: first for being born in the United States of America, a great country. For his late mother Beulah Mae Adkins Coleman Sealey Thomas, his late father Joseph James Coleman, his children, his family, and his many friends; he gave a special thanks for his wife of 21 years.

He also gave special recognition to his youngest child, Jozzlyn Janika Coleman who drew the art concept for the cover of the first printing of TAATA in 2001.

He is thankful to his oldest daughter, Meredith Coleman McGee, a second-generation author in his bloodline, for releasing the 2nd printing of TAATA via Meredith Etc, a small press, in Jackson, Mississippi.

PRAISE FOR TAATA

I read the book. I found it most interesting. In fact, it made me think about things that I have never before thought about. I recommend it very highly.

James H. Meredith, Author, Lecturer, Activist
First black graduate of the University of Mississippi
Jackson, Mississippi

Words for my fellow traveler Minister Coleman
TAATA will open readers to a perception of God that can be life changing. This book begins to break down the barriers of mind, body, and spirit. TAATA will guide you to the rebuilding of a right relationship with the Godhead.

Raymond Harris, Minister of the Gospel
Alpharetta, Georgia

My father always shared the word and light with me since I was a little girl. I was taught independent study and inner guidance... We are often deceived through our lack of understanding of the word. Let TAATA be a new guide to an old truth.

Willa Coleman Ridgway (Reya Peach), Poet, Songwriter, Recording Artist,
Jackson, Mississippi

CONTENTS

FOREWORD

Time And Time After Ahead: TAATA was originally released by my father, a bible scholar, before the rise of Print-on-Demand and e-books. He and my stepmother Catherine Dunn Coleman started BCII Publication at a time when self-publishers had to invest in boxes of books to get a discount on print copies. There were 25,000 self-publishers in the USA then compared to 1.68 million today.

My two younger sisters played roles in the publication of the first printing of *Time And After Time Ahead*. Daddy's knee baby, Willa Coleman-Ridgeland, wrote an endorsement, and his baby Jozzlyn Coleman who was a teenager at that time drew the art concept for the cover which included the moon, stars, and a clock.

The ancient Hebrew or Jewish calendar which was influenced by Israelite and Babylonian societies is lunisolar because it was in sync with the natural cycles of the Sun, the Moon, and the Holy Scripture. Use of the 13-month calendar dates to 780 – 850 CE. The months followed cosmological seasons; mathematical concepts were applied to ensure religious ceremonies occurred at the same time each year.

Our father was the first author in our immediate family. Today, there are three generations of authors in his bloodline. I, the eldest daughter, am an author and a book publisher. Daddy's only great-granddaughter, JaNiya Williams, became a published author at age eight in 2015; his granddaughter, Calla Ridgeway, Willa's daughter, is a published illustrator.

Years ago, daddy taught me how to make gumbo and our family's secret cold and flu syrup recipe which he learned from Grandma Christmas Eve. Fresh ginger roots, honey, red onions, lemons... are used to make the syrup. It works like a charm. Other families make similar solutions. Many call their homemade cold medicine hot totties. Daddy once purchased me a stove and gave it to me on Christmas Eve; the gift was not a Christmas gift because the only significance of the 24th of December to him is that his grandmother was born on that day in 1898.

Grandma Christmas Eve was in daddy's village teaching family traditions. Indeed, daddy was a special child. He was the first grandchild and the first nephew in his family line. This publication explores in part the shift of religious traditions and societal customs as governmental and communal rules changed.

A picture of Samarians on page 53 in the early 20th century wearing traditional head coverings, preparing a sheep carcass for the Passover Feast depicts people living in biblical lands carrying out ancient religious traditions. The men and boys were wearing kippahs. As is today, the young learn cultural norms from the old.

During biblical times, Samaria was in Central Israel between Galilee in the North and Judea in the South. Today, the Palestinian Authority refers to part of ancient Samaria as the West Bank. Moses dwelled in this land.

The carcass reminded me of Daddy's grandfather, Thomas Adkins, who was a butcher for a local grocer in Gadsden, Alabama during the Great Depression (1929-1939). Grandpa' Thomas's profession afforded him the opportunity to provide meat for his family when meat was scarce.

Grandpa Thomas and Grandma Christmas Eve are buried in the Ballplay Community, in Etowah County, Alabama. Daddy's side of the family celebrates May Day (Declaration Day) at the church site which was established by our family in 1883 in Ballplay, nearly 140 years ago. The community is called Ballplay because it is situated on the site where the Cherokees played ball game competitions before they were forced to relocate to Indian Territory via the Trail of Tears at the direction of General Andrew Jackson who became the 7th president of the United States of America in 1829.

Daddy is a Methodist who studied biblical history and the Hebrew religion under the tutelage of the late Rabbi Robert Devine of Florence, Mississippi. When we were teenagers in the 1970s, Rabbi Devine had a small service in his living room in West Jackson. He often wore a kippah. So, many onlookers likened him to be a Muslim rather than a Hebrew who practiced Christianity because Christians in western society do not typically wear traditional head coverings.

Daddy originally migrated to Jackson, Mississippi as a transfer student in 1959 on a football scholarship to attend Jackson State College. When my famous Uncle James and his first wife Mary June Meredith enrolled in college in 1960, they met daddy, a popular football linebacker, in the registration line and became fast friends. My uncle wrote a book endorsement too. He told me he was very proud of daddy because completing goals is important.

Daddy is a bible scholar who wore a kippah too. Before his health declined, he often quoted bible scripture like it *wasn't nobody's business*. He moved back to Jackson, Mississippi 10 years ago from Alpharetta, Georgia where he was a minister affiliated with the National Association of United Methodist Evangelists Worldwide Ministry among other organizations. Today, he enjoys listening to the word via audiobooks.

While **TAATA: Time And After Time Ahead** is a scholarly book, it is a very enjoyable read. This text will teach some and remind others that the Romans altered time when they replaced the Hebrew calendar with the Gregorian calendar and the Romans muddied religion when she added pagan rituals into mainstream Christian culture.

I implore individuals to read TAATA which contains pertinent biblical historical context and explores, at best, the dogmatic and lasting impact the Roman Empire (27 BCE – 1453 CE) had on Christianity.

Meredith Coleman McGee, Publisher, Meredith *Etc*
Jackson, Mississippi

Ra sun god, Egypt, photo by Carol M. Highsmith
Courtesy of the Library of Congress

THIS BOOK IS PRESENTED TO:

Encampment of the Aulad Sa'id Mount Sinai drawing
Feb. 18, 1839, David Roberts, R.A. 1845
Courtesy of the Library of Congress

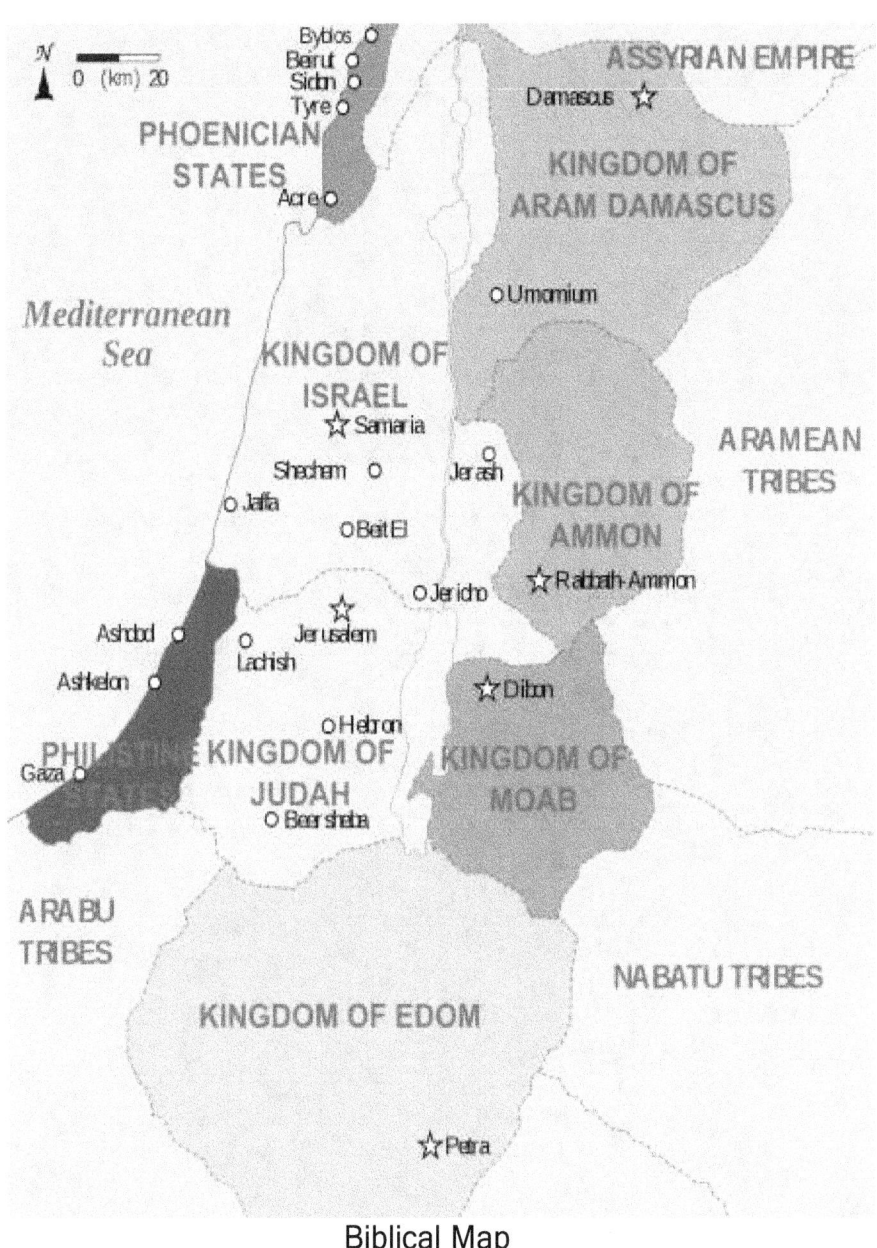

Biblical Map

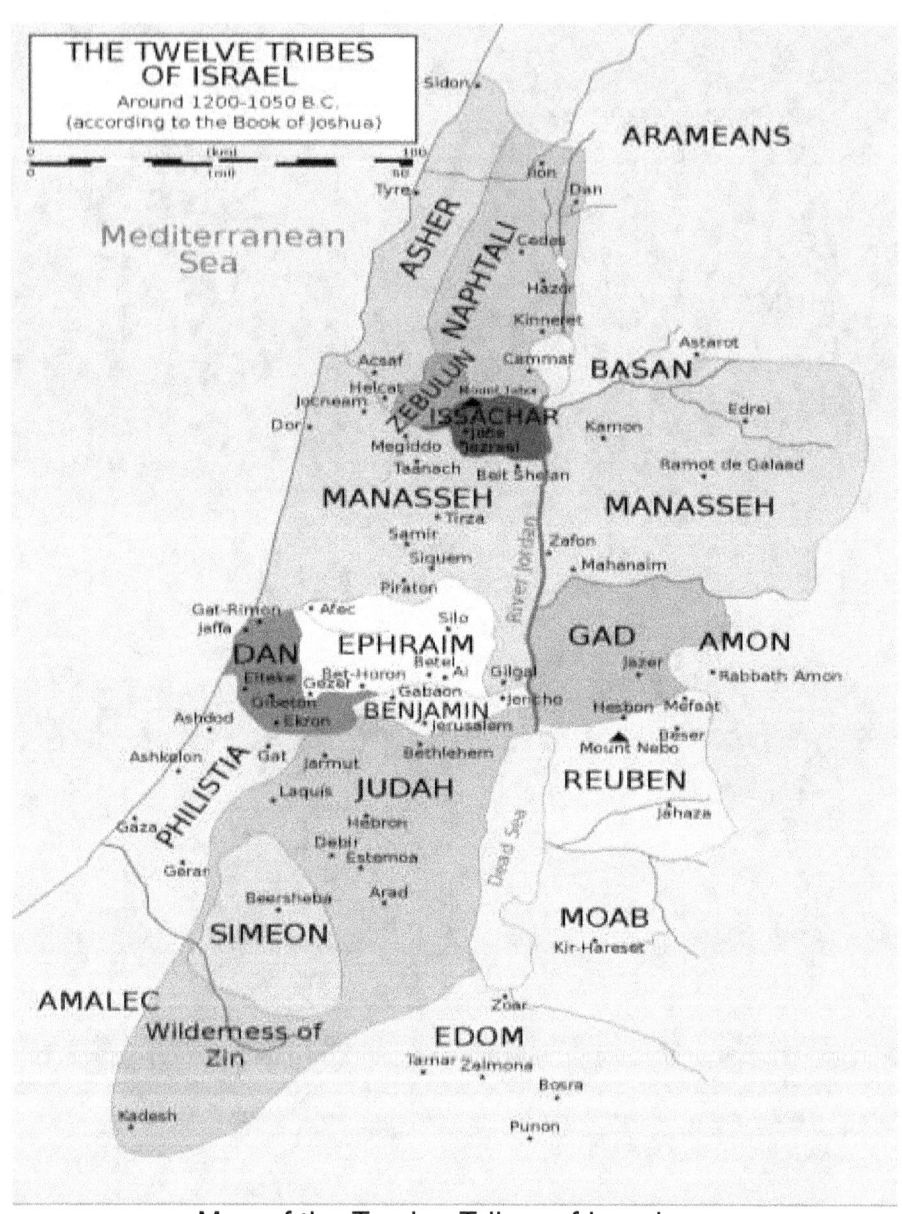

Map of the Twelve Tribes of Israel

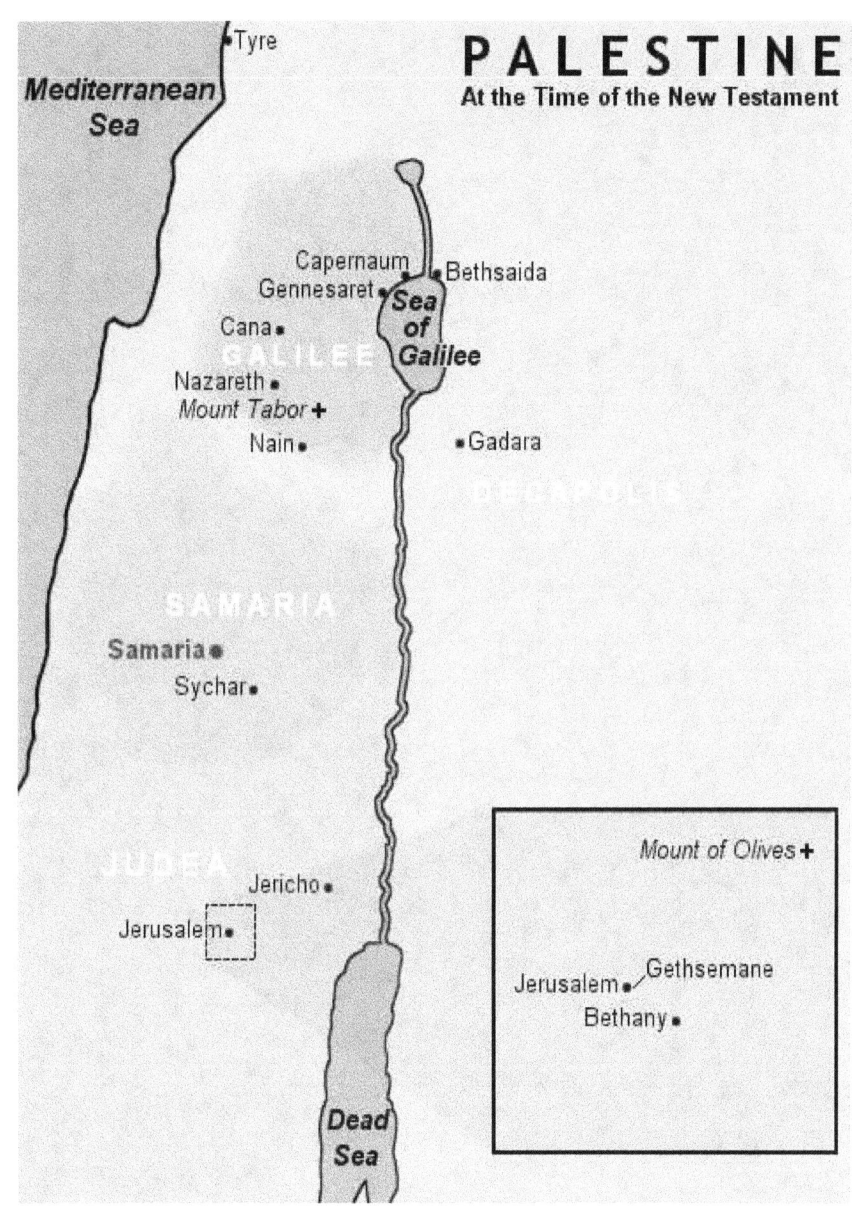

Palestine at the onset of Christianity around 10 CE

INTRODUCTION

One of the most difficult things to find in life is two or more people who have the same time of day. Timepieces, clocks or watches may differ from each other by one to ten seconds. Sometimes the time difference can be a matter of one or two minutes. This is accepted and understood by most people as keeping good time. However, if a person's timepiece differs with another's by one-and-a-half hours and they live in the same time zone, both individuals tend to become excited.

If there is a common intention to bring individual's time in line with the time of the majority of the people of their nations or civilizations, they will confer with others in the society, cooperate on setting the timepiece together, and then continue to go on with everyday life.

Today, almost everyone would agree that there are 24 hours in the day. In earliest Biblical time, the sun, moon, and stars were used as the determining factors of the time periods of days, months and years! For generation after generation, the sun, moon, and stars were used by mankind to broadcast the seasons as well as the time of day.

In the Holy Bible, the fourteenth verse of chapter one of the very first book states: And God said, "*Let there be lights in the firmament of the heaven to divide the day from the night; and let them be for signs, and for season, and for days, and years.*"

In the fifteenth verse: "*And let them be for lights in the firmament of the heaven to give light upon the earth: and it was so.*"

In the sixteenth verse: "*And God made two great lights; the greater light to rule the day, and the lesser light to rule the night; He made the stars also.*"

In the seventeenth verse: "And God set them in the firmament of the heaven to give light upon the earth."

In the eighteenth verse: "And to rule over the day and over the night, and to divide the light from the darkness: and God saw that is was good."

In the book of Genesis, the twenty-second verse of the eighth chapter states: "While the Earth, and cold and heat, and summer and winter, and day and night shall not cease."

In the book of Job, seventeenth chapter, eleventh verse, we are told: "My days are past, my purpose are broken off, even the thoughts of the heart."

In the twelfth verse: (Men) "They change the night into day; the light is short because of darkness."

The Babylonian day, as in most eastern countries, started at sunrise because the Babylonians believed in 'RA", the sun god. However, the most accepted Hebrew time of day began at sunset.

Sunset is referred to in the book of Deuteronomy, chapter twenty-three, eleventh verse: "But is shall be, when evening cometh on, he shall wash himself with water: And when the sun is down, he shall come into the camp again."

This instruction in very clear. This is part of God's law – an ordinance dealing with cleaning or washing time. The diver law is reproved or confirmed in the book of Nehemiah, fourth chapter, twenty-first verse:

"So, we labored in the work: and half of them held the spears from the rising of the morning till the stars appeared."

The ancient Israelites observed the three stars in the second magnitude, as these stars become visible. In that moment, dawn began with evening or shortly aftersundown.

This is based on the creation of God in the book of

Genesis, chapter one, verses 5b, 8b, 13, 19, 23, and 31b. Each verse repeats the same phrase, which came from the Holy Writ of the book written by Moses: "And there was evening and there was morning."

This book, TAATA, is not written for any reason other than to bring a serious focus to, and a basic understanding of, Christian error regarding time division as it related to the three world ages, with emphasis on the current age in which we are living now, contrasting men's tradition and doctrine as it relates to the Word of God through Jesus Christ. We ask you, the reader, the very most important question of your life ... which is nothing more than, "Brother, pardon me. Do you have the right time?"

CHAPTER ONE

It's About Time

The question is, can any man tell us when time started? We will not attempt to answer or respond to that question, although there may be some 'intellectual PhDs who may be under the illusion that they have the authority to do so based on their education.

We do know, however, that there are over 5,783 years of recorded history using Jewish records. We can put a lot of trust in the records, and the ancient 13-month calendar, with four weeks in each month for a total of twenty-eight days in a month: 13 months x 28 days = 364 days in a year. Today, later in time, of the history of calendars, there are more than 260 worldwide calendars in use. From the Gregorian Calendar around 46 or 48 B.C until sometime in the early seventeenth centuries, A.D., the Western World ended up with the imperfect Gregorian, old Julian or Roman calendar. In this, an extra day was added every fourth year to make up the few seconds lost every day.

The Jewish calendar is a perfect calendar with divisions of seven. There is a world belief that this "World Age" in the Western World has already been divided into two parts: B.C. and A.D. It seems incredible to us that there could be any person living today who does not know this time division. It is unbelievable to think that the whole western civilized world should be so mistaken about such an important thing as the time of day.

We can believe, however, that many people might not know much more – such as what "A.D." means. What does "A.D." stand for? In long hand it means "Anno Domini" a Latin phrase meaning, "In the year of our Lord." It is also known as "After the birth of Jesus Christ."

Common sense will tell all people that "B.C." is simply before the birth of Jesus Christ. Common sense should also tell us there are only twenty-eight days in a month. So, many believe, and a few know, that 7 days x 4 weeks = 28 days mathematically. Additionally, 28 days x 13 months = 364 days in a year. Historically, in the Gregorian calendar, an extra day was added to the only pure month, February. This happened every fourth year on what is called Leap Year.

In 1998, using the young Roman calendar, the month February begins on a Sunday, just as God started Creation. Thus, Sunday would be the 1st, 8th, 15th, and 22nd, with the month ending on Saturday, the 28th. How, then, can some nations talk about a fifth Sunday, or 2-3 other 5th-day anything of the month? Have you ever noticed when a four-and-a-half or six-year-old child is asked the question, "How many days are there in a week?" Before the question can be completed all the children will scream out, "It's seven days!" All the children will want to talk, and the real smart children will tell the teacher that there are four weeks in a month. Then, they might begin talking about that special day last week, usually referring to 'that other day." The teacher will go on and on.

Sometimes men and women are a lot like children whenit comes to listening to someone other than himself or herself. Few, if any, have time to listen even to the Word orthe Spirit of the Word, and will not be led by the inner voiceof their heart, mind and soul. Loose tongues – and closed- up ears – can sometimes cause us to lose sight of where wehave come from, as well as where we are going.

It is very hard to hear, with just your ears, what another is trying to communicate to you. There are even greater difficulties opening our hearts and minds to receive that which is communicated.

The last book of the Holy Bible contains one of the most important instructions given by the Angel of the Lord, and it has to do with listening (hearing). In the book of Revelation 22: 17-19 verses:

And the Spirit and the bride say, "Come. And let him that heareth say, Come. And let him that is athirst come. And whosoever will, let him take the water of life freely.

For, I testify unto every man that heareth the words of the prophecy of this book, if any man shall add unto this book, If any man shall take away from the words of the book these things, God shall add unto him the plagues that are written in this book:

And if any man shall take away from the words of the book of this prophecy, God shall take away his part out of the book of Life, and out of the holy city, and from the things which are written in this book."

Jesus Christ, the Angel of the Lord, made it very clear in those verses that doing, and hearing were both important as well as what the Spirit (and the Bride) say to us. That is the Commandments of God – the Word of God.

The Son of the Most High has given an instruction on first hearing and then for doing: to get a gift, a reward, water to drink (everlasting life).

In order to get the gift (eternal life), we must understand that the word of the only High God Almighty has been given to us by the prophets. The prophecy is inspired by the Lord God of Hosts. All we ever need to know, hear or understand has already been given to us by the Spirit of the Word in the Holy Bible. In order to hear, we must study, fast, and pray to

6

get the understanding of what the Word will say to each of us.

One or two verses taken out of context – which aperson begins to preach while using his own arrogantwords – will not lead to an understanding. No words oferror and lies will ever lead to understanding what God saysto us. Even a book of the Bible or prophet cannot give usthe complete path or correct direction to receive the reward.

Jesus, the man, and the last prophet of this world age said we must study the books of the law with the books of the Old Testament and the New Testament. When the "Holy One of Israel" walked on earth, he fulfilled all the prophecies written about him before he let mankind put him to death. He did not agree to making even one change to the law, scripture or the Jewish time system of 24 hours in a day, with the seventh day of rest, or any prophecy based on the three-world-age.

The pre-incarnated Logos, Jesus the Christ, testified to the churches (governments/nations) in relation to time, thatis found in the book of Revelation 23: 13 "I am Alpha and Omega, the beginning and the end, the first and the last."

Today, to verify the truth at a hearing in our courts system, one is required to be sworn in before testifying before jurors and judges. In our courts everyone must place their left hand on the Holy Bible, and by raising their right hand before God "swear to tell the truth and nothing but the truth, so help me God." Jesus knew this and that one day his testimony would be brought into question and cross-examined by skeptics of his words, "the Word of God." As the last judge, Jesus put himself on the witness stand oflife before the Church (nations/governments of the world age) by making a declaration of this world age; in the Holy Bible, to the believer, his friends, and to enemies as well.

Jesus is just as concerned about "the lost sheep of God" as he is about God's last day of rest. He taught the importance of the 24-hour-day, as well as one moment of an hour, event to a fraction of a second or the twinkling of an eye. As it related to his second coming, special days of a month, the Passover, and with common sense, a month that begins every year as well as the last day of the last month of each year. In so many words, it can be said that "the Angel of the Lord," "the Son of man," "Son of God," "the first born (begotten), "Zion (House)," "the Word of God," or "the Redeemer," is in himself before time of man, andbeyond the ending of man, and this world in which we nowlive.

In Isaiah 55: 5-13, we are told:

Behold, thou shalt call a nation that thou knowest not, and nations that knew not thee shall run unto thee because of the Lord thy God, and for the Holy One of Israel; for he hath glorified thee.

Seek ye the Lord while he may be found, call ye upon him while his near:

Let the wicked forsake his way, and the unrighteous man his thoughts: and let him return unto the Lord, and he will have mercy upon him: and to our God, for he will abundantly pardon.

For my thoughts are not your thoughts, neither are your ways my ways, saith the Lord.

For as the heavens are higher than the earth, so are my ways, and my thoughts than your thoughts.

For as the rain cometh down, and the snow from heaven, and returned not thither, but watereth the earth, and maketh it bring forth and bud, that it may give seed to the sower, and bread to the eater:

So shall my word be that goeth forth out of my mouth: it shall not return unto me void, but it shall accomplish that which I please, and it shall prosper in the thing whereto I sent it.

For ye shall go out with joy and be led forth with peace: the mountains and the hills shall break forth before you into singing, and all the trees of the field shall clap their hands.

Instead of the thorn shall come up the fir tree, and instead of the brier shall come up the myrtle tree: and it shall be to the Lord for a name, for an everlasting sign that shall not be cut off.

There is no one who has ever lived on earth who was able to walk in and out of time as they pleased, other than Jesus Christ. When Jesus was in the flesh, walking on earth in a terrestrial body, He made an astounding statement. He said that He God the Father, that is greater than He, Jesus Christ, showed him what he had to do, having sent him, himself (Jesus). No one, not even He himself (Jesus) knew the end of time, only the Father. Because of this we trust only in God and worship God.

Time as we know and live in this world age only relates to man. Because of this, mankind has limits in this life. Men and women, sometimes knowing that there is such a small amount of time given to us by Almighty God, often waste too much of the time given them by our Father God by doing nothing.

Keep in mind that God only gave his own son, the Christ, 33 years to develop from a baby to become the greatest man ever to live. We say to ourselves that we have time on our hands and accuse others of the same. Does this mean that we have time to do something tomorrow or give us some kind of unwritten law of excuses" When we are very young, it appears we never have time to do everything we want to do each day. As we become older, we think to ourselves we never have time to do anything. As we become older, we think to ourselves that time has gone by so fast, that it was just yesterday we did so and so. At class reunions, we confront each other with the question, "Can you believe it? It has been 40 years...!"

At the end of the world age B.C., Before Christ, the very start of the second part of the world age, A.D., there is a lot of misleading information written by man about the books in the Bible and the history of western civilization, theRoman Empire, as it relates to Jesus Christ.

According to Jewish tradition, the B.C. world age started more than 5,783 years ago. Babylonian myths boast of two great world leaders who both lived more than 3,200 years ago, before the great flood. Egypt had a great sun god, "Ra," and adopted the goddess, or their Queen, "Ishtar." According to the legend, Ishtar, fell from the clouds as an egg out of the water onto land, where it was hatched by a dove. The goddess, Queen Ishtar, emerged. Thus, an event known now as Easter was celebrated to honor Ishtar.

The Roman Empire accepted some of the myths from Babylon and Egypt, which they mixed with the Word of God. Greek mythology, with all its gods and goddesses, was under Roman control and world domination for more than 400 years. When anyone went against the law of the Roman Empire, the punishment was instant death.

Myth, religion and history have western and eastern history in agreement about many things relating to the time periods of B.C. and A.D. The exact timing of this period of change varies according to which history or government is accepted. Man's time starts 75,000 to 1,000,000 years ago - more than a few seconds. You can say: "What a difference a day makes."

Amazingly, the end of the B.C. period and the start of the A.D. period, using Jewish records, would put a number around 5783 (less 1999). Depending on which government's history is accepted, Jesus the Christ's year of birth can differ by as many as five to seven years before hisbirth, or three years after. According to Jewish records, there was very little time in the changing over, unless his gestation period is considered.

Jesus told Nicodemus that man must be born of water before he can be reborn of the Spirit. The divine plan of God is to have every soul he sends to earth be born of water for his terrestrial body. I Corinthians,15: 37-58 states:

> And that which thou sowest, thou sowest not that body that shall be, but bare grain, it may chance of wheat, or of some other grain:
>
> But God giveth it a body as it hath pleased him and to every seed his own body.
>
> All flesh is not the same flesh: but there is one kind of flesh of men, another of beasts, another of fishes, and another of birds.
>
> There are also celestial bodies, and bodies terrestrial: but the glory of the celestial is one, and the glory of the terrestrial is another.
>
> There is one glory of the sun, and another glory of the

moon, and another glory of stars: for one-star differed from another star in glory.

So also is the resurrection of the dead. It is sown in corruption; it is raised in power:

It is sown a natural body; it is raised a spiritual body. There is a natural body, and there is a spiritual body.

And so, it is written, the first man Adam was made of a living soul: the last Adam was made of quickening spirit.

Howbeit that was not first which is spiritual, but that which is natural; and afterward that which is spiritual.

The first man is of the earth, earthy: the second man is of the earth, earthy: the second man is the Lord from heaven.

As is the earthy, such are they also that are earthy: and as is the heavenly, such are they also that are heavenly.

And as we have borne the image of the earthy, we shall also bear the image of the heavenly.

Now this I say, brethren, that flesh and blood cannot inherit the kingdom of God: neither doth corruption inherit incorruption.

Behold, I shew you a mystery: we shall not all sleep, but we shall all be changed,

In a moment, in the twinkling of an eye, at the last trump: for the trumpet shall sound, and the dead shall be raised incorruptible, and we shall be changed.

B.C., before Christ, does not mean that he was not there

during B.C., because we believe Christ was one of the "Us" when God said: "Let us create man and divide light from darkness," in the book of Genesis, chapter one.

In the Holy Bible book of John, first chapter, verses one and two state: "In the beginning was the Word, and the Word was with God. And the Word was God. The same was in the beginning with God."

The true B.C. or A.D. is found in Luke 1: 41-45:

And it came to pass, that, when Elisabeth heard the salutation of Mary, the babe leaped in her womb; and Elisabeth was filled with the Holy Ghost;

And she spake out with a loud voice, and said, "Blessed art thou among women, and blessed is the fruit of thy womb."

And whence is this to me, that the mother of my Lord should come to me?

For, lo, as soon as the voice of thy salutation sounded in mine ears, the babe leaped in my womb for joy.

And blessed is she that believed: for there shall be a performance of those things which were told her from the Lord.

John knew who Jesus was the moment, Mary, mother of Jesus, came in the presence of he and his mother – even when John was just six months in Elizabeth's womb, after the Holy Spirit sent God's spirit for the conception. John knew that this Holy one was Jesus.

As a baby boy, John was no smarter than any other child. The main difference was John and Jesus both were born of the Holy Spirit; first John and Jesus both were born of the Holy Spirit; first John with the spirit of Elisha, and then Jesus with the Holy Spirit of God. After nine months, when Mary's water broke, Jesus came out from the water as flesh, man of God. The time of his birth signals the changeover from B.C. to A.D.

CHAPTER TWO

Second Magnitude

As American Christian believers of the Word, we never hear sermons on the subject about the time of day – preachers, teachers, and pastors do not talk about the difference of time of day. Preachers, teachers, and pastors do not talk about the difference of time of day. We know, however, that there are noticeably big differences in the eastern and western nations.

In the east, the difference is as much as night and day. There is a clear difference between a Babylonian day and a Jewish (Hebrew) day. Babylonian - and most near-eastern nations – start their day at sunrise. The ancient eastern nations had many gods; one was the sun god, a favorite to the Egyptian and the Babylonian people. The Roman nation, perhaps, was the first of the western modern political powers to start a new day at 12:00 midnight.

When Jesus had to deal with the subject of time of day, he made it truly clear that the time of his Father, God, and his earthly father, was the time he taught from. This was the time handed down from creation based on the creation account, which had been well established by the Hebrew prophet, and the prophecy of six days of creation and the seventh day of rest. He had very little to say about the eastern nation days, maybe for two reasons. Neither Egypt nor Babylon was in power during his sojourn and terrestrialvisit with the use of the Heavenly Body movement of sun, moon, and stars. This time was spiritually different for thesenations through use of some common sense in the startup of their day.

Rome was in power then, and Jesus made fun of the

Roman day, in the book of Mark, 13:35. He called the Roman time of day unpredictable and asked a question about whether it was the time of the cockcrow or midnight. He made it clear that no matter what time man used, the last watch – "that day" of the end – was only known by God the Father.

The six-day creation account, and the seventh day of rest of God, - the early Hebrew time – is the only time that has been tested and proven as the time when Jesus walked on earth as a terrestrial being. Now, in today's world age, we are going into the last phase of time as we know it.

Mankind is still out of touch and step with God's time. Some schools - even seminary schools of theology - teach a theology that has gone far beyond the Word of God. For example, there is scripture which states that one day to man is a thousand years to God, or a thousand years to man is one day to God. This scripture has been taken out of context. Jesus made it clear that there are 12 hours in a day and 12 hours in a night. It is an error for these schools to take this thousand year out of context and not accept the six-day creation account as having 24 hours per day. God did not make days for himself; he made days for mankind to give order and stability to his creation.

This is clearly demonstrated by Jesus's announcement regarding the relation of time or hours to a day. It is not with mankind's so-called common sense, but rather with the law and commandments of Spirit, of the Word, that which is God. Now, because of the Spirit, we of this world age know there should be 12 hours of darkness and 12 hours of light in each day.

For theologians, governments or nations to interpret a day as years – at creation in Genesis – is a gross error. This is remarkably close to taking sides with the biggest liar of

all time
Satan, the false morning star - and disbelieving the bright star.

To those who believe and the few who know, when God created the earth, He created heaven as well. In the very beginning there was gross darkness – a void – and then the Spirit divided the night of darkness from the day of light. The very first day was a sun day. Maybe this is why we callour first day of the week Sunday. Generation after generation, the first day has always been known by the dayof the sun.

There is one big problem with all this Sunday, first-day thing. In accordance with the Word of God, the first day started in the evening as God intended, and each day in creation – the second, third, fourth, fifth, and sixth – all started in the evening. They all started with the three stars in the heaven of the Second Magnitude.

God knew He had to keep his creation plain and simple. Mankind always makes a big deal out of everything and anything God has given him. Modern theologians will rationalize homemade ideas, and to try to come up with a new way of talking about Sunday – special days or God's Word and ways – without having the fortitude of calling God a flat – out liar.

We have always had to accept these homemade, manmade theories, because they are connected to each other and sometimes rise to positions of authority andpower with man. They psych each other up, referring to each other as "Doc," "Good Doc," or "Heavy Doctor." These 'good, heavy doctors' of men sometimes write papers and books with their theories differing just a little bit from the Word of God's Holy Plan. We have had to put up with this foolishness and have been lulled to sleep.

In Genesis, the first book of the Bible, the first chapter,

and the fifth verse read as follows:

"And the evening and the morning was the first day."

Verse 8, "the second day:" verse 13, "3rd day;" 19th verse, "4th day;" 23rd verse, "5th day;" and 31st verse, 6th day." These repeated phrases, which come from the Holy Writ in the early Hebrew writings, read as:

"And there was evening and there morning."

After creation, every time a new day began in the evening, three stars would be seen shortly after sunset – after the dawning of that day. Dawn ended as soon as these three stars became visible, and the next day started in the evening. The second magnitude let the entire world know that the order of God is for mankind's benefit, and this God is for mankind's benefit, and this is God's own pleasure made by him.

The stars, moon and sun were all made two days before man and three days before the holy day of rest for God. So, on the fourth day, the sun, moon and stars were made by God. Evening and morning and confirmed in The Holy Quran, in the record of the birth of John the Baptist and Jesus. Zacharias wanted a sign to assure himself that in his old age, with his barren wife, he would have a son as God instructed the angel to bring good news of John's birth. The fourth section:

He said, "O my lord
Give me a sign."
"Thou sign," was the answer
"Shall be that thou
Shall speak to no man
For three days
But the signals
Then celebrate
The praises of the Lord

18

Again, and again,
And glorify him
In the evening
And in the morning."

In the German Holy Book, Die Bible, Einheits
ubersetzung: Die Bucher Genesis is one of the five books
written by Moses:

(Diefunt Bucher des Moses)
(die sie Tora Gesetz)
Das Buch Genesis
I Chapter Verses 5B
ES Wurde Abend,
Und es wurde
Morgen: erster tag.

The West, including the German people and the East,
have both been given the Holy Word of God about a day
that began in the evening, and then morning with the first
day, and each day starting in the evening and then morning.
Very few, in any, have seen a Roman Bible. It would be
interesting to see if the account of creation of God's first day
started at midnight or what? The whole western world the
old "Roman Empire," once again, has taken chapter of
Revelation, tenth verse, we are told:
I (John) was the main reason or justification for the
empire to call the Lord's Day Sunday. Before we accept this
falsehood, we must study the subject. The subject was in a
"spirit dreamlike-vision state of mind:" the Roman military
leaders had killed all the other prophets outright, but with
John they wanted him to die a slow death, exiled on an
island of rock. This was meant to be funny to the Romans.
This arrogant, vain act might justify the early acceptance of

the day of the sun (Sunday pagan) from the Babylonian. You cannot justify the pagan sun god practice with the only true Lord's Day. The Babylonian astrologers were the first sun god worshippers to divide the calendar into a seven-day week. Every day was changed into another name, except Sunday.

Last, and most importantly, Jesus, by his example, led the Jewish believers to continue to observe the Sabbath, the seventh day of rest of God! Another factor was the early belief of the east and now the west; "Ra" in the Egyptian delta as well as the other names solar (Atum Kephri) and reviving of the old early name for the sun (Aton).

This happened before Abraham left the city of Ur, so it seems possible that Abraham knew about sun day and the sun gods, as well as the seven-day week calendar. What we do know is that Abraham worshipped the moon, which led God to smile on Abraham's faith in just one part of God's creation.

God converted Abraham's faith in the moon into faith of the Living God himself, Jehovah. The Roman Empire's error was in trying to make the Lord's Day Sunday, just as much as the whole western world is in a great position of error, darkness and maybe death and Hell itself with misunderstanding of Jesus's own words, when he said, "I am the Lord of the Sabbath," as recorded in Matthew: 12: 1-8:

> At that time --- went on the Sabbath day through the corn; and his disciples were an hungered, and began to pluck the ears of corn, and to eat. But when the Pharisees saw it, they said unto him, Behold, thy disciples do that which is not lawful to do upon the Sabbath day. But he said unto them, Have ye not read what David did when he was an hungered, and they that were with him; How he entered into the House of God,

and did eat the shewbread, which was not lawful for him to eat, neither for them which were with him, but only for the priests?

Or have ye not read in the law, how that on the Sabbath day the priests in the temple profane the Sabbath, and are blameless? But I say unto you, that in this place is one greater than the temple. But if ye had know what this meaneth, I will have mercy, and to sacrifice, ye would not have condemned the guiltless. For the Son of man is Lord even of the Sabbath day.

No Christian in the western world has ever challenged the "Roman Empire" during the 400 years of unholy rule of the world, and very few do so now in relation to the 'lie' that the resurrection of Jesus was on Sunday morning. In Mark, when Mary went to the tomb, Jesus was already gone before Sunday morning. This was also recorded as being the case in both the gospels of Luke and St. John.

The problem with all of this is time of day in every case. In Matthew, we will not bring this up again in relation to the Lord's Day, Sunday, because this is our final warning to fools and non-believers and believers alike in the book TAATA.

In the book of Matthew, 28: 1, the Resurrection is spoken of:

"In the end of the Sabbath as it began to dawn toward the first day of the week came Mary Magdalene and the other Mary to see the sepulcher." This creates problems with trying to squeeze in Sunday morning at this time of day. Jesus is already gone; she was gone too. This is written by a Jewish young man, Matthew, who was with Jesus every Sabbath day for more than three years. In the end of the

Sabbath, the Word tells us it is still the seventh day just about sundown on Saturday. Mary Magdalene and Mary were no different from most of us today. We do not go to the graveyard at night and, because they were good Jews,they knew the law about the Sabbath and the secondmagnitude. The time is dawning on Saturday, with no mention that it is dark enough to see the three stars. It did not say, "and the evening and the morning were Sunday, the day of the week."

Jesus is still very much the Lord of the Sabbath. There has never been a Passover like that Passover. Why, you ask? On the first Sabbath, the Saturday before this man who was talking about Jesus, we will call that Sabbath #1. Now let us talk about the other Sabbath. We will call this Sabbath #2.

We who know by the Spirit know that the 2nd Sabbath started that Tuesday night at sundown, after the dawning and the three stars in the second magnitude became visible. The Passover meal was eaten, and Jesus took his men to a field for them to watch out for him to pray, early in the evening of the mid-week. This second Sabbath was a high Sabbath, coming every 40 years, representing the 40 years of Israel in the wilderness lost, but under the care of God himself.

On this Sabbath, Jesus was tried, convicted and crucified after enduring a lifetime of pain and suffering. The Bible talked about three time periods. The Bible talked about three time periods. The third hour, which according to the Roman and western world time would be about 9:00 a.m., was one of those periods. He is on the 'tree' – the Roman term for 'cross.' – at the sixth hour, which would be 3:00 p.m. Roman and western world time is 12:00 noon when the sun is at its highest refer to as "broad open daylight.' However, when Jesus gave up the ghost, the earth split into,

22

it was dark, and the dead walked for a while.

The first Sabbath was on a Saturday; the second Sabbath was on a Wednesday. Thus, the Word of God is true because on Wednesday – at the ninth hour Jewish time or 3:00 p.m. Roman time – Jesus went into Hell or graves to take away death's sin from Satan. From Wednesday – the fortieth year Sabbath ninth house, or 3:00 p.m. Roman time – Thursday at this very same time is twenty-four hours. Friday at the same time would be forty-eight hours or 3:00 p.m. Roman Time is the last great Sabbath depending on how much time we as believers think in our hearts it took Jesus to straighten out hell, Satan's kingdom.

When the false preachers in the west teach or preach that Jesus died on Friday night, so called Good Friday, and rose early Sunday morning, that is Satan's way of holding onto the stupidity of a false doctrine or mankind. Jesus never lied while he walked on earth, so when he spoke about Jonah and the whale, and the three days he would be in the earth, his own and last prophecy about his life on earth was fulfilled by himself, with this reward – that Jesus would take the seat at the right side of the throne of Almighty God.

East of the Jordan and Dead Sea. Corinthian capitals of the Temple of the Sun [Jerash]. American Colony (Jerusalem). Photo Dept., photographer 1900-1920

CHAPTER 3

Holidays of Man

What we are about to say in this chapter may make people angry. If, however, you want to live when you die, we implore you to read, hear, and understand what the Word of God and the Spirit will tell you by the Word of Almighty God Jehovah.

Every holiday of mankind, without exception, is vain, arrogant and pagan! Mankind or Satan celebrates anything that is wicked. For example, the loss of blood of some people or nations at their hands. We understand this kind of holiday. The victory dance is as old as time itself. In this book, we are not concerned with minor national or regional holidays. For example, America's Thanksgiving holiday. These holidays may or may not send people to hell. However, the main, worldwide holidays, which violate God's Holy Word and commandments, will be taken up in this chapter of TAATA.

In order to talk about a holiday, one must understand this: that just as there are different times of day with the startup of each day with the startup of each day with all nations, there are governments and nations with different months that start a new year. The Hebrew calendar extends from the events prior to the flood up to Abram then onto Moses and leading into the present. The Hebrew calendar records 1,999 years after the birth of Christ A.D. and some 3,500 to 4,000 years before the birth of 'Jesus the Christ.' It is all based on the creation account of Almighty God.

By no means is this part of TAATA intended to be a quick history fix from the book *The True Blue Jew* by

Azhreal Yusuf Bin-Israel. We know that there are 3,333 years plus more time with the Jewish calendar over the old Roman calendar. The defunct Roman calendar was replaced by a somewhat imperfect Julian calendar some 44 to 48 years before the birth of 'Jesus the Christ," the Son of God.

The Roman and Julian calendars struggled for 1,400 years before they realized that time is important mathematically. The Emperor, Julius Caesar, and the other Caesars changed the 28-day calendar to have more days in the month that bore their names. For example, the seventh month Roman calendar to July, 31 days from 28 days, August 8th month, October 10th month, December 12th months and so on etc. After hundreds of years of this vain madness, the Roman Senate outlawed the naming of months after emperors. They kept February a pure 28-day month, and then started the 12-month calendar.

Then, however, came the church that was to improve on the Roman calendar. So, in A.D. 1582, under the Pope rule, their Gregorian calendar superseded the Julian and Roman calendars. England, in 1752 A.D., fell in line, along with the rest of the western world. Once an attempt was made to communicate this fact of time to a Christian believer, the response was typical of the thought process of a "born again Christian" – you know – the ones who think they are saved through their own spirit and self-righteous hearts.

A true believer was instructed by Paul, the New Testament writer, that is was good to have learned with the Spirit. He said that we first should try that Spirit, with the Word of God, because there are all kinds of spirits, before the throne of God under the control of Jesus Christ, and the Holy Spirit of Jehovah. Revelation: 1:3-5:

Blessed is he that readeth, and they that hear the words

26

of this prophecy, and keep those things which are written therein: for the time is at hand.

John to the seven churches, which are in Asia: Grace be unto you, and peace, from him which is, and which was, and which is to come; and from the seven Spirits which are before his throne;

And from Jesus Christ, who is the faithful witness, and the first begotten of the dead, and the prince of the kings of the earth. Unto him that loved us, and washed us from our sins in his own blood.

Paul declared the spirit is good to have, but a believer needs the knowledge as well as the Word of God, through Jesus the Christ the Word of God. "Why," you ask, "does it matter that nations start their year with different months?" Most western nations start the year on the first of January of each year. Some eastern nations start in the spring or early summer. For example, the law that was given to the early Hebrews, or Israelite Jews, by God, started in what the west calls April. The name that the Jewish people call April is "Nisan." Pope Gregory instituted the month with a new holiday, "April Fool's day."

The prophecy warns us that man would know when a new year began with the budding trees, flowers and the bees and birds. In other words, God made the trees and green things for signs of the seasons as he did with stars, the sun and the moon. In the 12th and 13th chapters of Exodus, the first five of six verses of each chapter, God spoke to Moses and Aaron that the month of Abib, or April, should be the first month of the year to Israel forever. Moses did not tell God or ever ask God about this. This was a commandment from God.

27

Now, to answer your earlier question, it does matter what – and which month – starts each year off every year.

First: "God said it,"

Second: "Most of the Old and New Testament was written by Jewish prophets."

In the fourth chapter of St. John in the Bible, Jesus talked to the woman at the well. She and her family didn't know what they were worshipping, because God is a spirit. Those who worship God should worship him in spirit and in truth, because God is a spirit and his word is truth. Jesus also made it clear in this chapter, when he said that salvation is of the Jews. This statement cut long, wide and deep. First, because God is the Word and Jesus is the Word of God. Second, the Jewish people never got rid of the Ten Commandments or the Eating Law, and Living Ordinances, which they passed on to the entire world – God's Word to the utmost parts of the earth.

One place where misunderstanding has been caused in the western world is in the first chapter, twenty-sixth verse of St. Luke. This is where mention is made of Mary receiving Jesus on, or in, the sixth month of the year.

We watch many TV Christian teachers and preacherswho try to justify Jesus' birth on the 25th of December. Once, a good teacher even proclaimed that he knew the moment and the day that Jesus was conceived. He used the 24th day of December so he could still believe in Christmas.We never utterly understood how he came up with his findings, but ever he questioned himself!

It does not matter that Jesus was not born on a certain day. In the days that he lived, he did what God sent him to do. It is the work and Word that Jesus did that is the most important thing. However, when we pay attention to the

28

command from the 12th and 13th chapter of Exodus, it should be clear that with God's word the first month is April.

Thus, using the Jewish thirteen-month calendar or the ridiculous Roman calendar, the sixth month would have been September. You don't have to be a rocket scientist to know that nine months later, Jesus would have been born in what we in the western would call June. Somewhere in our research, we were told the Roman Empire churches wanted to keep the Old Babylonian customs of celebrating the reincarnation of Nimrod from the grave as a tree. God was angry at his people in Jeremiah 10: 10-13:

> But the Lord is the true God, he is the living God, and an everlasting king: at his wrath the earth shall tremble, and the nations shall not be able to abide his indignation.

> Thus, shall ye say unto them, the gods that have not made the heavens and the earth, even they shall perish from the earth, and from under these heavens.

> He hath made the earth by his power, he hath established the world by his wisdom, and hath stretched out the heavens by his discretion.

> When he uttereth his voice, there is a multitude of waters in the heavens, and he causeth the vapours to ascend from the ends of the earth; he maketh lightning with rain, and bringeth forth the wind out of his treasures

Legend had it that this Babylonian king married his own mother so that she would remain Queen. After the death of Nimrod, a tree grew in or on top of his grave. The Queen, his mother, made everybody pay a tax on the little idol. In addition, everyone had to have a tree in his home and in the temples. They were told that Nimrod was a god in the form of a tree.

Babylon, oh' Babylon.
What is truth?

So again, the Roman Empire would please all the sun god worshippers by mixing something old with something new: the 25th of December – first Christmas- Nimrod-birthday-with-our new-savior-the-birth-of-Jesus-Christ-son- of-God. We don't know what to believe. Rome, Babylon: "What is true? Oh' where is truth?"

Note: (taken from *The True Blue Jew* by Ahzrael Yusuf Bin-Israel).

When we study or investigate the Word of God in Jeremiah 10: 2-5:

Thus, saith the Lord, Learn not the way of the heathen, and be not dismayed at the signs of heaven; for the heathen are dismayed at them. For the customs of the people are vain: for one cutteth a tree out of the forest, the work of the hands of workman, with the ax. They deck it with silver and with gold; they fasten it with nails and with hammers, that it move not. They are upright as the palm tree, but speak not: they must needs be borne, because they cannot go. Be not afraid of them; for they cannot do evil, neither also is it in them to do good.

God said that mankind was always looking for signs in heaven that were not there. For example, some of the psychics or palm readers and fortune-tellers use the zodiac signs. He said man is like dumb oxen when it comes to not believing in truth by holding on to vain doctrine of falsehood.

The big problem with nations in the western world, or the old Roman Empire, is that they like to get a quick fix – something that does not require study or just hearing the Word of God. Jesus knew that Christmas would be associated with his birth and Easter his resurrection. There are just two more reasons why he kicked over the money tables of the moneychangers then, and now, with the Word.

Once Jesus was asked by tricky teachers and lawgivers why worked on the SABBATH. His answer was given with power and authority for the future believer then, now, today, tomorrow and forever. Jesus said, "I am the Lord of the Sabbath." Luke 6:5.

Why mankind is still unbelieving in Jesus's word is beyond spiritual understanding, as the whole western world is under the leadership of the Roman Empire, which is the father of lies and falsehood ministers of Satan. There has never been a time in Hebrew history, Christian history, Roman, Greek, Egyptian or Babylonian mythology when the whole world was given proof of the Word of God, at the last Passover Sabbath, that Jesus conducted while he terrestrially lived on earth.

TAATA would like to have you know that the Word of God will not accept the falsehood, lies and wicked words of Satan. Satan was not accepted after the fast of 40 days by Jesus then, and God will not accept him now. All lies that mislead people are punishable by an eternal death of fire forever, with every unbeliever and Satan the father of death and sin. The day of judgement by Almighty God and the army of heaven under the command of the Lord of the Sabbath - Jesus Christ, Son of God, King of Kings, and Lord of Lords will do this.

When we travel back in time with the Word of God, more than 1,998 plus years with the life and ministry of Jesus, we find works that the eastern and western world witnessed. All prophecy was fulfilled concerning Jesus and the time we are living in now. One prophecy by the prophets about Jesus was that he would be killed on a mid- weekday, a Wednesday.

In the book of John, the eighteenth and nineteenth chapters refer to this day as a high Sabbath, or the mid-week Sabbath. It was a fortieth-year Sabbath given to the Israelites for the remembrance of the fortieth year that God took care of all the people after being in the wilderness 40 years. This was the Exodus from Egypt when God guided his flock for 40 years: feeding, cleaning, and giving them his law in the form of the Ten Commandments.

Jesus hung on that tree from 12:00 noon mid-day on a mid-week until the hour of 3:00 o'clock p.m. midway between the light of day and the darkness of night. By the grace of God, through the Son of God, Jesus fulfilled the mid-Sabbath with his crucifixion. At that same moment, the temple "Veil" (two curtains) was rent (split) in half by the new veil – the Lord of the Sabbath, the House. The new church met God in the temple of the Lamb of God, the spiritof truth, that is love, and the Word of God.

On the first Sabbath of this Sabbath Passover, Jesus kept the Hebrew tradition of teaching every seventh day on the holy day of God's creation, which begins in the second chapter of Genesis. On the third Sabbath, the last Sabbath of the three Passovers, the resurrection of Jesus started a new church government, in which he is the 'House" or temple in which to worship God Jehovah.

There will never be another celebration as that three Sabbath Passover with Hebrew Jewish tradition. Neither will there be any accepted myths of the pagan goddess Ishtar (from Babylonian and Egyptian eastern world) Venus and Queen Diann, the Greek goddess, queen of western old-world Roman Empire.

Satan was unable to make Jesus serve and worship him during Jesus's weakest time, after the 40-day fast, Jesus put Satan in his place – behind him. Satan used scripture to persuade Jesus to follow him. This proved that even the Devil himself knew that the Word of God was Jesus's protection. However, like some teachers, preachers and Christians – Satan added a little white lie to God's truth. But, Jesus knew that Satan was taking God's words out of context. Jesus warned that when you add to or take away from God's Word, you seal your own path.

In the New Testament of the Bible, the first four books – Matthew, Mark, Luke and St. John talks about the last days of Jesus, his ministry, the truth, the fulfillment of all prophecy with his crucifixion, and his resurrection to everlasting life with the power of Almighty God. The western world always uses the books of Mark and Luke to justify keeping the 3500 B.C. Ishtar (celebration) Roman Easter, and sun god pagan day of sun-god worshipers: for keeping "Sunday" and the first egg rolling "Queen of Heaven." What was introduced in Babylonian myth ended up in Greek andRoman "Venus" other pagan myths.

The reason so many people are misled by this action is that the small-minded leaders of government and churches are ignorant of the Word of God – his truth. These leaders are more into tradition and doctrine with church employers – employment, job relationships, money, the so-called 'good life' – even if it means the loss of their souls.

Secondly, they are misled by more than 400 years of world rule with no respect for life and love. It is a civilization that produced fear and Satan's true world government. Each book in the book including Mark, Luke, and sometimes St. John, speak of different times of day, as well as different people finding out that Jesus Christ had risen from the grave.

Thirdly, and most importantly, they are misled by the vanity and arrogance of mankind without the Spirit and the knowledge of the Word of God. Study, Prayer and Truth are here, if we would only open our hearts to hear what the Spirit says to each and every one of us.

Matthew must have known about the resurrection first, as seen in 25:1: "In the end of the Sabbath, as it began to dawn toward the first day of the week came Mary Magdalene, and the other Mary to see the sepulcher."

As to which day this is, one must understand that the writer is a Jew (Hebrew). The key statement is not just the Sabbath – seventh day or Sunday the first day, but "As it began to dawn toward the first day of the week."

The Roman day is ruled out, because the Roman day starts at mid-night. There is no dawn at this time of day; plus, Jesus made fun of this absurd time in the Mark 13. So, by ruling mid-night out, that leaves only two other times of day with the dawning: the Babylonian day at sunrise, or the Hebrew day at sunset.

Common sense indicates what Jesus would have said that we should work in or while it is the light of day, not darkness. Even if you did not have good mother wit, or common sense, truth is on the dawning of a day. The law ofa day is given at creation, by God. The moment that the dayends, and a new day began after the dawn is over, and in the darkness the three stars can be seen in the 'second magnitude.'

CHAPTER 4

Lota; Jot, Tittle

In the fifth through the tenth chapters of Matthew, in the King James Version of the Bible, Jesus began his teaching with the Sermon on the Mount – the how tos, who-dos, the whens, whys and whats – that must be done for God's children to enter into heaven, the kingdom of God.

By the Spirit of God, Jesus gave us instruction concerning the light of the world and so much more understanding of truth with the Word and the Spirit of God. In this chapter of TAATA, we want to take up something very important as it relates to a so-called new theory of the western world Christian beliefs or pagan habits.

In Matthew 5:16, Jesus said: "Let your light so shine before men, that they may see your good works, and glorify your Father which is in heaven." It is noted that Jesus was true to this word with his crucifixion and his resurrection. The world saw then in broad daylight, this death, and his rising before the dawning on one day, and the darkness of the evening of the pagan first day of the week 'sun tag.'

Believers can be sure that Jesus would never have us hear truth, the Word of God, and then do something altogether different. Matthew 5:17: "Think not that I am come to destroy the law, or the prophets: (a better spiritual term prophecy). Jesus said, "I am not come to destroy, but to fulfill."

Matthew 5:18: "For verily I say unto you, until heaven and earth pass, one jot or one tittle shall in no wise pass from the law, until all be fulfilled.

Note: "That day," – The Lord's Day, the second coming of Jesus Christ - has it come? We as believers are watching, and as the old Negro spiritual song says, "waiting for that great getting up day." This lyric, based in slavery, had two meanings. The slave-masters thought the slaves were singing about the second coming of Jesus. The song, however, had a hidden cry to God for freedom from slavery as well. We, as true believers, know that this prophecy is from the last great prophet of all – Jesus the Christ.

Matthew 5:19-20:

Whosoever therefore shall break one of these least commandments, and shall teach men so, he shall be called the least in the kingdom of heaven: but whosoever shall do and teach them, the same shall be called great in the kingdom of heaven.

For, I say unto you, that except your righteousness shall exceed the righteousness of the scribes and Pharisees, ye shall in no case enter in the kingdom of heaven.

Jesus made it very clear in these verses that the law is still the law. He made no changes to the law. However, he did give the western world, the New Age Christian believers, a warning. Here again, Jesus emphasized the importance of following what the commandment told us to do. This was as important as knowing what the commandments were. He further warned us that by not doing what we were instructed to do would lead to us to not being called into heaven. It seems plain and simple that if we are not permitted to enter heaven, that only leaves one other placeto go – and that's hell.

We must develop a mature understanding, respect and

fear for the Word of God. King Solomon exemplified respect for God. I King 3:10-15 states:

And the speech pleased the Lord, that Solomon had asked this thing.

And God said unto him, Because thou hast asked this thing, and hast not asked for thyself long life; neither hast asked riches for thyself, nor hast asked the life of thine enemies; but hast asked for thyself understanding to discern judgements;

Behold, I have done according to thy words; lo, I have given thee a wise and an understanding heart; so that there was none like thee before thee, neither after thee shall any arise like unto thee.

And I have also given thee that which thou hast not asked, both riches, and honour: so that there shall not be any among the kings like unto thee all thy days.

And if thou wilt walk in my ways, to keep my statutes and any commandments, as thy father David did walk, then I will lengthen thy days.

And Solomon awoke; and, behold, it was a dream. And he came up to Jerusalem, and stood before the ark of the covenant of the Lord, and offered up burnt offering, and offered peace offerings, and made a feastto all his servants.

God gave Solomon wisdom; why would Solomon be brought up in this part of TAATA? Understanding and knowledge is needed to be in the Spirit and the Word of God. We need to speak about a man that pleased God in his response to questions by God. Solomon wrote papers and books. We are going to focus on some of his writings.

Proverbs 1:1-7 states:

The Proverbs of Solomon, The son of David, King of Israel;

To know wisdom an instruction; to perceive the word of understanding;

To receive the instruction of wisdom, justice, and judgement, and equity;

To give subtilty to the simple, to the young man knowledge and discretion.

A wise man will hear, and will increase learning; and a man of understanding shall attain unto wise counsels;

To understand a proverb, and the interpretation; the word of the wise, and the dark sayings.

The fear of the Lord is the beginning of knowledge; but fools despise wisdom and instruction.

These were written by Solomon in the first chapter of Proverbs, and in the sixth chapter, verses 16 - 23. Proverbs 16: These six things doth the Lord hate: yea, seven are an abomination unto him 16:17:

1. A proud look,
2. A lying tongue,
3. And hands that shed innocent blood,

Proverbs 18-23:

A heart that deviseth wicked imaginations, feet that be swift in running to mischief,

A false witness that speaketh lies, and he that soweth discord among brethren;

My son keep thy father's commandment and forsake not the law of thy mother.

Bind them continually upon thine heart, and tie them about thy neck.

When thou goest, it shall lead thee; when thou sleepest, it shall keep thee; and when thou awakes, it shall talk with thee. For, the commandment is a lamp, and the law is light; and reproofs of instruction are the way of life.

The new western world theology – and the most dangerous doctrine of mankind in any of the three world ages – is happening now with the peace and love doctrine: Do what you want to do! God loves us, and Jesus has already saved us. True! Yes, it is true. That it is written in the Bible, "God loveth," and we are saved by the Blood of the Lamb of God! With the Spirit, and the Word of God, Jesus the Christ, Son of God. All these statements are true, and very real, and they are important statements. Oh! by the way, we forgot to include the most important condition – the biggest, and most used "little word" in the King James version – 'If'. There are over 1,594 times that 'if' is used, with love, save, salvation, and commandment law, etc.

The new world age (order) still lets (Satan) take a big truth and mix it with a "little small white lie," by leaving the most important teaching or things that Jesus said in the Bible: "If you love me, you would or will do my father's commandments. There is not one theologian, or any place in the New or Old Testament where it is written that Jesus got rid of the law.

The saved and born-again Christian – by man's tradition and new doctrine – believers, have been indoctrinated to think and incorporate into their seminary, schools, church denominations and almost the entire western world the belief that Moses wrote the ten commandments. After the death of Jesus, the Christ, and his resurrection, Jesus did away with commandments. This is a false doctrine. Hold on here a minute! Are we missing something in the tenth an eleventh chapters of Exodus? Exodus, 10: 20-23: verses say:

But, the Lord hardened Pharaoh's heart, so that he would not let the children of Israel go.

And the Lord said unto Moses, stretch out thine hand toward heaven, that there may be darkness over the land of Egypt, even darkness which may be felt.

And Moses stretched forth his hand toward heaven; and there was a thick darkness in all the land of Egypt three days:

They saw not one another, neither rose any from his place for three days: but all the children of Israel had light in their dwellings.

Stop! Look and Listen! As Paul, the writer of the New Testament, would ask, "How be it?" Did you notice, who said what to Moses? How about this three-darkness day thing here? We can only say that the gates – and possibly the chambers surrounding the Egyptians – are hell. Almighty God once again is in control and, on top of everything that pleases or displeases him, Jehovah.

How about that other thing, the darkness being so thick that they could feel the darkness? We don't know about you, but "that's heavy." Take a real close look at these verses. He divided the light from the darkness. During those three days the Egyptians are in complete darkness. Israel was in the light. After the Lord had fulfilled his will and power, he told Moses that he, Jehovah, had one more plague – which was the big one. "The mother of plagues" the death at midnight; the start of Satan's new day. And the beginning of a new day for God's people. In the eleventh chapter of Exodus, ninth and tenth verses:

And the Lord said unto Moses, Pharaoh shall not hearken unto you; that my wonders may be multiplied in the land of Egypt. And Moses and Aaron did all these wonders before Pharaoh: and the Lord hardened Pharaoh's heart, so that he would not let the children of Israel go out of his land.

True, Moses transcribed all the things that God inspired and instructed him to write. So, it is true that Moses transcribed only that which had been spoken by God. Exodus 19: 3-8 says:

And Moses went up unto God, and the Lord called unto him out of the mountain, saying, Thus shalt thou say to the house of Jacob, and tell the children of Israel:

Ye have seen what I did unto the Egyptians, and how I bare you on eagles' wings, and brought you unto myself.

Now therefore, if ye will obey my voice indeed, and keep my covenant, then ye shall be a peculiar treasure unto me above all people: for all the earth is mine:

And ye shall be unto me a kingdom of priest, and an holy nation. These are the words which thou shalt speak unto the children of Israel.

And Moses came and called for the elders of the people, and laid before their faces all these words which the Lord commanded him.

The question – and the big answer – is: what do we think the children of Israel would have said to Moses aboutthe Lord's request? Do we think that the children of Israel are any different from us today? If this had happened to us today, is it any different from us today? this "midnight-and-light-and-darkness thing," how many would tell God 'no'? God was not surprised that these new, born again Jews would say 'yes' to his request? He was not through with his new children.

From the author's point of view, there is a very new revelation to us in these verses of Exodus in the nineteenth chapter. We believe that the forty-day fast that Jesus performed before he started his ministry is directly rooted and founded in the very first three verses of Exodus, chapter nineteen.

Further, there is this three-day phenomenon. We know that earlier, some forty days prior to the time of this event, God had given Pharaoh a three-day total darkness in which we stated that this was hell! Also, this is the third month of the year, and if we were to use the western world Gregorian calendar it would be what we call June. It is amazing, and incredibly powerful, and divine authority that Christ Jesus – Blood of the Lamb- is in everything here in this scripture. That is the root and the origin of light over darkness and heaven over hell or death – Satan.

Moses only did that which God instructed him to do. For

in the next few verses, we discover the most important truth of the commandments and the law. It is not just the Word of God or the spirit of God. It is the power and the fear of his voice. Exodus chapter 19: 9-11 noted:

> And the Lord said unto Moses, Lo, I come unto thee in a thick cloud, that the people may hear when I speak with thee, and believe thee forever. And Moses told the words of the people unto the Lord.
>
> And the Lord said unto Moses, Go unto the people, and sanctify them today and tomorrow, and let them wash their clothes.
>
> And be ready against the third day: for the third day the Lord will come down in sight of all the people upon Mount Sinai.

When we thoroughly study these verses, we understand and realize first that the fear of the Lord is the beginning of all knowledge. The children of Israel were so afraid of the voice of God, that they made a request of Moses; that God would not speak unto them. Secondly, the forty-year wilderness encampment of Sinai began here in these scriptures. It is significant that Jesus the Christ was nailed to the cross on the forty-year Passover Sabbath, which has been celebrated by God's people from this foundation of God's divine plan! Thirdly, why would Jesus change any of his father's commandments and law?

In the very beginning, it is written:

"LET US DIVIDE THE LIGHT FROM DARKNESS."

Matson color slides and filmstrips of Bible Lands, by Matson Photo Service (photo taken 1950-1977... Family - primitive irrigation system

CHAPTER 5

The Great Connection

Almighty God, -- Jehovah or YHWH" – our heavenly Father, gave the earth a promise to the first believer, and father of the nations of this world age we live in now. YHWH God loved King David, even before David was crowned king of Israel, and Judah. The great connection began with the father of all the world nations. Our heavenly father promised Abraham that the world would be blessed through his seed. This is the start of the covenant continued through 28 generations to King David, there are many theological sermons preached throughout time about the "little babe." David against the giant Goliath. The modern theological debate symbolized that Goliath represents the kingdom of Satan. A lot of this debate was based on the fact that Goliath had six fingers on each hand, and six toes on eachfoot, forming the revelated symbol of '6666.' However, this was really a symbol representing what was to come, ofthe final world age before the Regeneration of Jesus Christour Lord and Savior.

The Goliath and David story in the Bible is based on the premise referencing the love of God for his greatest patriot, David. King David started the great connection when God promised David that he would be great, like unto the rest of his fathers in the earth. David, in scripture, asked if he could sit at the right-hand side of God's throne. We know God loved David so much because he did not chastise David. God knew that David honored and loved his father Jehovah as chapter, 1 Chronicles 17:10-27 said,

And since the time that I commanded judges to be over

my people Israel. Moreover, I will subdue all thine enemies. Furthermore, I tell thee that the Lord will build thee an house.

And it shall come to pass, when thy days be expired that thou must go to be with thy fathers, that I will raiseup thy seed after thee: and I will establish his kingdom.

He shall build me an house, and I will stablish his throne forever.

I will be his father, and he shall be my son: and I will not take my mercy away from him as I took it from him that was before thee.

But I will settle him in mine house and in my kingdom forever: and his throne shall be established for evermore.

According to all these words, and according to all this vision, so did Nathan speak unto David.

And David the king came and sat before the Lord, and said, Who am I, O Lord God, and what is mine house, that thou hast brought me hitherto:

And yet this was a small thing in thine eyes, O God; for thou hast also spoken of thy servant's house for a great while to come, and hast regarded me according to the estate of a man of high degree, O Lord God.

What can David speak more to thee for the honour of thy servant?

O Lord, for they servant's sake, and according to thine own heart, hast thou done all this greatness, in making known all these great things (I Chronicles 17:19).

O Lord, there is none like thee, neither is there any God beside thee, according to all that we have heard with our ears (I Chronicles 17:20).

And what one nation in the earth is like thy people Israel, whom God went to redeem to be his own people, to make thee a name of greatness and terribleness, by driving out nations from before thy people, whom thou has redeemed out of Egypt?

For thy people Israel didst thou make thine own people for ever; and thou, Lord, becamest their God.

Therefore now, Lord, let the thing that thou hast spoken concerning the servant and concerning his house be established forever, and do as thou has said.

Let it even be established, that thy name may be magnified forever, saying, The Lord of hosts is the God of Israel, even a God to Israel: and let the house of David thy servant be established before thee,

For thou, O my God, hast told thy servant that thou wilt build him an house: therefore they servant hath found in his heart to pray before thee,

And now, Lord, thou art God, and hast promised this goodness unto thy servant;

Now therefore let it please thee to bless the house of thy servant, that it may before thee forever: for thou blessest, O Lord, and it shall be blessed forever (27).

Because David had so much faith in God, when it came to defeating the army of the Philistines, led by the giant Goliath, God took him from following the sheep and made him king of his chosen people Israel and Judah. When we read 11 Samuel 7: 8-11, and 12 (twelfth is the key verse) verses we can follow David's journey:

> Now therefore so shalt thou say unto my servant David, Thus saith the Lord of hosts, I took thee from the sheepcote, from following the sheep, to be ruler over my people, over Israel:

> And I was with thee whithersoever thou wentest, and have cut off all thine enemies out of thy sight, and have made thee a great name, like unto the name of the great men that are in the earth.

> And when thy days be fulfilled, and thou shalt sleep with thy fathers, I will set up thy seed after thee, which shall proceed out of thy bowels, and I will establish his kingdom (12).

The prophet Nathan reproved the purpose of David in 11 Samuel. Nathan, like Samuel the prophet, was inspired by God through prayer, and daily communication with the father. This was not Nathan's idea to prophesy about what would happen in the end of this world age, about the seed of David. It was the inspiration of Almighty God himself – the great "I am that I am!" The God of Abraham, Isaac and Jacob. Nathan, being a good prophet with all obedience to the holy spirit, did that which God instructed him to do, to not only tell David what God wanted him to know, but also what God wanted him to do. Some theologians are very confused about this chapter, for later God, through his prophet Nathan, talks about a house, or temple and a son that will have an everlasting relationship with God, and be his son forever. The book of Isaiah prophesied about the Abraham and David covenant. In Samuel, the foundation for our Lord and Savior Jesus Christ – and the great connection for the kings of kings and Lord of Lords – is established. This is the beginning of the kingdom of God, in heaven, and on the earth.

In the first chapter of Luke, verse twenty-six, this event has been prophesied almost from the very beginning of time that a virgin would be with child that was conceived by the Holy Spirit. Fourteen generations prior, in second Samuel, God had given instruction to the prophet Nathan about this delicate 'seed' this holy thing. The earthy seed that will bring a terrestrial son with the holy spirit, and to bring the heavenly seed of the son of God. There have been many errors in Christian theological seminary teaching and church organizations in western world theology. This is partly due to the counsel at Nicaea, held sometime at or between 325 A.D. Here, a bunch of boys who ordinarily would have been recognized as gentile heathens made the decision as to how the world should refer to Almighty God and our Lord and savior Jesus the Christ, and the holy spirit.

This doctrine may have been responsible for what we call in the western world the Holy Roman Church, and the holy trinity. The council decided as well what substance God was, is, and what substance Jesus is, and if there is a difference or likeness with the three: the God, the Son, and Holy Spirit. Is it possible, for understanding by the holy spirt, that learned or unlearned atheists, lawgivers, professors, and weak theologians can determine what the difference of I am that I am, the king of kings and the lord oflords, the great I am, Alpha and Omega, first and last, and the beginning and the end? The answer is "yes, no and no!" Yes, the council did make this decision or created this document, - which has thrown the western world into an erroneous religious state of being – based on undocumented principles, traditions and doctrines that are not the Word of God!

When we read in Matthew that Jesus was asked by some of his followers which commandment was the greatest or most important, Jesus answered and said that the greatest commandment is to love thy father, Almighty God, with all thine heart, might and soul. Jesus made it very clear thatthe laws of Moses explained in detail who his father Almighty God is, and what honor, and position of power, that our heavenly father has. Jesus then asked his followersa question: "Have you not read 'for it is written?'" And straight from the book written by Moses, Jesus made a reference to Deuteronomy sixth chapter, fourth verse: 'Hear, O Israel: the Lord our God is one Lord."

Jesus never questioned, doubted or changed the law and commandments of God, which had been spoken by God and later transcribed by Moses, who had been inspired by Jehovah to do so. Therefore, the answer to the question as to whether the Council at Nicaea can determine whom God is, what substance he is and whether there is a trilateral God or only God is an absolute no! There is no way these atheists make that decision! Was the counsel right on any part of their document? Again, the answer is no!

This answer is not subject to any theological debate or Christian traditional doctrine or concern – just as Jesus forbode his disciples from making three temples on the mountaintop of his transfiguration with Moses and Elias. Peter asked permission to build three temples, one for the great prophet Elias, the great lawgiver Moses, and one for Jesus Christ. The voice of God came out of his cloud and spoke to the disciples with words of trembling and fear – so much fear that the disciples fell on their faces and had to be brought back to a terrestrial state of consciousness by Jesus Christ. How then can the modern western church declare all manner of undocumented traditions and doctrines that elevate the subjects, and son of God, to the same level of authority of God? Even our lord and savior Jesus Christ declares that until the end of time men should be cautious, that they do not trust in the angels above or below, but rather trust only in Almighty God.

In Luke, the first chapter, verses thirty to thirty-three, the promise and the great connection are fulfilled, and we find also authority is established with the promised seed of David. "And the angel said unto her, Fear not, Mary: for thou hast found favour with God. And, behold, thou shalt conceive in thy womb, and bring forth a son, and shall call his name Jesus. He shall be great and shall be called the son of the Highest: and the Lord God shall give unto him the throne of his father David: And he shall reign over the house of Jacob forever; and of his kingdom there shall be no end."

These verses make it clear that Jesus Christ is called the son of God, with the word and the announcement of one of God's most trusted archangels. Why then? In the scripture, Jesus will be given the throne of his father God, and yet in the tradition of man and the religious theology of the church and its governments, why is he not given the throne of his father David? Could it be just as there is doubt and many questions about the virgin birth of Jesus with Mary, that there can also be questions and doubt about the relationship of Jesus Christ the lord from heaven and king David seed of earth, forming that wonderful holy thing the son of God? Jesus Christ therefore it can be said, is only son of man and son of God even to live here on earth, in both terrestrial and celestial forms at one time. In the sixteenth chapter of Matthew, Jesus asked his disciples who did man say that he, Jesus, was? They all agreed that no one really knew who he was, for he had been confused with John the Baptist, Jeremiah, Isaiah or one of the prophets. Jesus referred to himself as the son of man. Everyone knew that Jesus was a man – a terrestrial being. It is obvious that he reminded people of other great prophets of the earth who were men. In the same breath that the disciples had declared that he looked like, or maybe did things like these prophets, there was still another side to the son of man. Jesus asked a most important question: "But whom do you say that I am, son of man?" Peter immediately answered, "Thou art the Christ, the son of the living God." Jesus confirmed this statement and said, "Flesh and blood did not reveal this to you Peter. For this is revealed by the father."

In Matthew earlier, the disciples asked Jesus, "Should we pray or how should we pray to you, Master?" Jesus answered them by saying; that they should only pray to the father, not only should they pray to the father, but he also gave them an example of how to pray, and what to the words to use in their prayer.

In the final chapter of Revelation, the very last book of the Bible and part of the last verses of scripture, we find in Revelation 22: 8-9:

And I, John saw these things, and heard them. And when I had heard and seen, I fell down to worship before the feet of the angel which shewed me these things.

Then saith he unto me, see thou do it not: for I am thy fellow-servant, and of thy brethren the prophets, and of them which keep the sayings of the book: worship God.

Jesus again instructs John, the writer, to not worship

him, but to worship God. The scripture goes on to declare that men who work and are led by the Word will be rewarded by Jesus Christ, because his reward is with him, to give every man according to his works. Finally, Jesus explained just who he is in the Revelation 22: 14-16:

Blessed are they that do his commandments, that they may have right to the tree of life, and may enter in through the gates into the city.

For without, are dogs, and whoremongers, and murderers, and sorcerers, and idolaters, and whosoever loveth and maketh a lie.

I, Jesus, have sent mine angel to testify unto you these things in the churches. I am the root and the offspring of David, and the bright and morning star.

The Samaritan Passover, Mt. Gerizim. Preparing the carcass.
G. Eric & Edith Matson Photograph Collection, 1900-1920
Courtesy of the Library of Congress

CHAPTER 6

Sun-god vs. Son of God

The Babylonians and most early eastern nations worshiped many gods. One of the favorite gods was Ra. Sun god. We as believers in the world age, in which we are living, know that there is only one true God, Yahovah. All the other gods have been proven to be fake, wicked, powerless and evil, paganistic myths about idols. We first discovered this: that Almighty God is the power and glory in the first five books of the Bible, written by Moses. We find the very first battle, holy or unholy war of the God of heaven with the pagan idol sun god Ra, according to Moses the law-giver, and commandment writer of Genesis, and Exodus. The Egyptians were under the rule and authority of the Pharaoh, who dominated the Israelite Hebrew people for many years and helped Egypt become the most powerful nation during their time of dominance. Like Rome, no one dared to question anything the Egyptian's Pharaoh wanted to do, to say, and even to think. This nation had begun to be so brutal, ignorant, vain and evil to God's chosen people.

It is written in Exodus that after Moses had been expelled from Egypt as one of Pharaoh's greatest military leaders, that the God of heaven, Jehovah, decided to use Moses to communicate to Pharaoh and the Egyptians about just how angry the Egyptians had made almighty God Jehovah. In the past or early Egyptian's history, the Pharaoh and Egypt were mighty and strong. No nation or any individual for more than four hundred years would challenge the authority of Egypt, and especially Pharaoh. History has never been clear as to just how the Pharaohs defied themselves with their idol gods.

The scripture talks about a time period of about forty years, and a fasting of forty days by Moses on the mountaintop in the presence of Almighty God. There is also a common belief among knowledgeable Christians that the son of God was also present on this mountaintop. Jesus Christ acknowledged that he was there to protect Moses from the consuming fire, as well as protecting the three Hebrew boys from the flaming furnace, and Daniel in the lion's den. When Moses had been prepared to give Pharaoh God's demand, "Let my people go," Pharaoh's reaction was typical of a king, emperor, or a ruler of a nation.

Egypt had a new Pharaoh, the son of the Pharaoh that ruled when Moses was a military hero in Egypt. According to scripture, the new Pharaoh not only knew Moses, they had a kind of brotherly relationship. At one time, Moses was the son of the older Pharaoh's sister, and the new Pharaoh was the son of the older Pharaoh. One can say that the new Pharaoh and Moses were in the same household. It was only natural, that Pharaoh would not respect Moses's new God.

First, the Children of Israel – the Hebrew people – also believed the God of Moses. Second, Pharaoh's god, Ra, was a gigantic huge statute representing the sun god Ra. Everyone saw Ra, and people could identify with him because he was a physical image. When Moses told Pharaoh about his new God, the God of heaven, the God of Abraham, Isaac, and Jacob, Pharaoh laughed. After many exchanges between Pharaoh's magicians and God's newest messenger Moses, the scripture reports that God instructed Moses to warn Pharaoh, or advise him, that Jehovah knew him before Pharaoh was placed in his mother's womb. God instructed

Moses to tell Pharaoh that Almighty God had made Pharaoh great before he was ever born, so that very minute God could exercise his power and authority forever.

Speaking off the record – not with the Word of God or commandment, but with common sense - I believe Pharaoh really did not believe in Ra but, because of the relationship of his idol god, and in his mind his supreme rule and authority, Ra and Pharaoh was one in the same. So, Pharaoh is the author of this war, between his idol Ra and Moses's new God Jehovah.

The writing of Moses clearly showed mercy and patience for Pharaoh and the Egyptian people. Pharaoh was determined not to let Jehovah God's people leave Egypt, since they were slaves. Pharaoh could not see Jehovah when he looked in the mirror. He saw himself, and when he looked at his giant idol Ra, he saw himself also. Even when Moses warned Pharaoh that God would deliver the children of Israel out of Egypt, Pharaoh felt his god Ra, and his power would prevail. Pharaoh, great king of Egypt, could not be told what to do, or how to do anything.

Even after many plagues were put upon Egypt by the staff of Moses, which were ordained by the father, Jehovah, Pharaoh still resisted. He even resisted when all the water was turned to blood, and Ra had blood running from his mouth, eyes and ears. This incident was symbolic, since Ra was not flesh and blood but was rather wood and brick. Blood cannot flow naturally from anything made of wood and brink. God had to give Pharaoh something to see that he could relate to – his idol god being defeated and bleeding to death.

Pharaoh had no compassion for his god when, in reality, he really thought himself superior to Ra. Pharaoh was so angry, he decided he would kill the first-born of every man, woman, child and beast of the Hebrew people. Moses had already warned Pharaoh that whatever he had in his heart, and whatever he planned to do to the Hebrew children, God would reverse it and do it to him and his people. It is obvious there is no real power with the sungod or any dictator, emperor, or even a great Pharaoh, when there is a confrontation with Almighty God. How could mankind still hold onto sun god practices, or pagan idol beliefs, then ... or especially, or pagan idol beliefs, then... especially, now?

There was never a real battle since the sun god was nothing then – he was void, empty and powerless and worthless. All knew Pharaoh's sun god was useless and worthless. All Pharaoh had his own image, and his own power. Upon the defeat of Ra, Moses warned Pharaoh one final time that if he did not do as God said and"Let my people go," God would do to him what he had in his heart.

In the Bible, there is reference to the word Passover. There are more than 76 times that Passover is mentioned in the scripture, in the Old Testament and the New Testament. The very first Passover happened on the night that Pharaoh defied God's instruction, "To let his people go." Moses had his friends and companions of the children of Israel sprinkle blood from a pure sacrificial lamb on their gatepost, and doors. This was symbolic of the Lamb of God, son of God, Jesus Christ Lord and Savior.

In biblical history, (twelve o'clock" midnight is a time of death. For the angel of death was sent through the land in Egypt, and the first-born of every man, woman, and child who did not have blood of the lamb for their salvation died at midnight. Every first-born of Egypt – even Pharaoh's first-born son – died at midnight, but thanks be to God, the blood of the lamb saved every soul of the Hebrew Israelite people.

How can modern man think or even imagine that any pagan form or custom can replace an act of God? An example of this is the very first Passover for his chosen people with a pagan holiday, called Easter. Easter is only mentioned one time in the entire Bible. That one time was a wrong translation from Greek. The translators should have used Passover dinner. The mistranslated use of the word 'Easter" crept into the Word of God, not by the spirit of the Word of God, but by ignorant men.

The Lamb of God is written about in the Bible from Genesis through Revelation. We know about the angel of death in Egypt at midnight in Exodus 11:4-7 which reads:

And Moses said, Thus saith the Lord, About mid-night will I go out into the midst of Egypt:

And all the firstborn in the land of Egypt shall die, from the firstborn of Pharaoh that sitteth upon his throne, even unto the firstborn of the maidservant that is behind the mill; and all the firstborn of beasts.

And there shall be a great cry throughout all the land of Egypt, such as there was none like it, nor shall it be like itanymore.

But against any of the children of Israel shall not a dog move his tongue, against man or beast: that ye may know how the Lord doth put a difference between the Egyptians and Israel.

So, because of incredible ignorance in the western world, under the influence of the Roman Empire, has chosen to start each day at midnight! Not only is this holding onto a time of death, but also a very horrible defeat of RA, the sun god, by the Creator. There is error trying to start a new day at midnight. Hold on! Not only have we started a new day in error, we have even gone so far as to substitute God's holy Sabbath with the pagan day sun-tag, the German word of Sunday. The author can understand mankind making a mistake by starting every day off wrong, losing sight of Saturday, the Sabbath. This is an exceedingly small period - a minute and six days.

Our research shows that there are two other reasons that the East had an eight-day week. At one time, the Greeks in the West had a six-day week. How in the world can we in the western world excuse errors of a giant time period such as the first month of the year, Abib; April, Nicea? The twelfth chapter of Exodus and the thirteenth chapter of Exodus clarify all of this. Even if we had a problem with not accepting the Passover and first month covenant from Exodus, then we should at least look at when Jesus instructed his followers to just read the law given by Moses in Deuteronomy m16: 1-3:

> Observe the month of Abib and keep the Passover unto the Lord thy God: for in the month of Abib the Lord thy God brought thee forth out of Egypt by night.

> Thou shalt therefore sacrifice the Passover unto the Lord thy God, of the flock and the herd, in the place which the Lord shall choose to place his name there.

> Thou shalt eat no leavened bread with it; seven days shalt thou eat unleavened bread therewith, even the bread of affliction; for thou camest forth out of the land of Egypt in haste; that thus mayest remember the day when thou camest forth out of the land of Egypt all the days of thy life.

We hate to keep hitting a sore spot, however, so please forgive us for pouring salt in the wound of this modern tiny pagan image with this final comparison of the errors in months. The original ninth month of the Jewish calendar Chisleu is found in Nehemiah 1: 1-4:

The words of Nehemiah the son of Hachaliah. And it came to pass in the month Chisleu, in the twentieth year, as I was in Shushan the palace.

That Hannai, one of my brethren, came, he and certain men of Judah: and I asked them concerning the Jews that had escaped, which were left of the captivity, and concerning Jerusalem.

And they said unto me, The remnant that are left of the captivity there in the province are in great affliction and reproach; the wall of Jerusalem also is broken down, and the gates thereof are burned with fire. And it came to pass, when I heard these words, that I sat down and wept, and mourned certain days, and fasted, and prayed before the God of heaven.

For the life of us, will someone in the western world please explain how the western world made a quantum leap of fasting and praying in Nehemiah, the first chapter, to celebrating Santa Claus in this same month? We know that with Gregorian calendar the twelfth month, known as December, is the same month that the Jews refer to as Chisleu, the ninth month.

CHAPTER 7

Regeneration

We originally wrote this seventh chapter in TAATA prior to man's so called two-thousand-year millennium. In order to get a most vital and crucial word from God to you the reader, we ask for your patience. We knew the Y2K computer bug was simply going to miss the mark. To expect anything to happen in prophetic terms involved the same arrogance shown by the leadership in the western world that tried to make the fake, defunct western Gregorian calendar, the accepted worldwide calendar. We must clear up the matter of the wrong time of day, the wrong time of month, and now the wrong thousand years!

Early in the 1830s, there was a sick young woman. History does not clarify whether she was mentally or physically ill. The main point of this is the beginning of misinformation, or non-understanding of God's Holy Word written in 1 Thessalonians, and later in II Thessalonians by Paul, the Jewish Hebrew eunuch New Testament writer. A whole new religious concept, or rather religious error, was born. There were two ministers or theologians at the bedside of this sick little girl. She had a nightmare about people flying. Sometime later, however, these two ministers used her nightmare to throw the western Christian world into religious disarray and frenzy.

These two religious leaders mixed this little girl's nightmare with the mistranslated definition of I Thessalonians, regarding when the Lord would come back. The leaders believed that He will meet us in the air, just as the translators have misinterpreted and did not investigate what the Greek meaning of air is, as opposed to Webster, Faunt, and Wagner or other new English dictionaries. These events create misunderstanding of the nonexistence of what they call rapture and born again. The definition for air in I Thessalonians should have been breath of life. Throughout scripture there have always been this term breath of life. In Genesis, when God breathed into Adam's nostril the breath of life, and it further stated that Adam or man became a living soul.

Back to Paul, the New Testament writer. In I Corinthians 15: 39-52, the scripture distinguished between death and life, spirit being a terrestrial earthy being. This error is symbolically the same as the virgins with no oil when their husband or master is returning to provide a light for them to be together. The rapture is a combination of a nightmare, and an ignorant error. "Born again" – the term used most loosely by American and sometime western Christians – is also a profoundly serious error. The true meaning of "born again"should be born from above. The modern western world is lost in ignorance.

The pagan Sunday, the New Western World empire, sprouts this erroneous message of peace and salvation. All this because we learned how to spell Jesus's name, and we sometimes just shout and call our J.E.S.U.S. Pharaoh could not save himself, nor could he save his first-born son, or any of the first-born men, women, children, or beast in Egypt.

History, in the early twentieth century, as it related to another world leader was problematic. Everything he said in his speeches, in his writing, in his meeting with his military staff, always connected him with what he thought was the divine sovereignty of God. Somewhere between 1939 A.D. and 1999 A.D., we have come to an understanding that

Adolph Hitler always stated in his speeches – even in his book "Mine Kampf" that PROVINCE would have him (Adolph Hitler) to do such and such. In his heart, he honestly believed he was saving the German people from spies, western imperialism, colonialism, and those people he felt were not the true Jews of God's chosen people. By no means is this a history lesson about Hitler and Pharaoh.

However, there is a comparison between people on the move either being part of Israel or claiming to be Jews. Pharaoh had no respect for the slaves of Egypt who were called Israel. Hitler as a young boy was raised as Jewish by his father and his father's people. Our research indicates that Hitler associated Judah with blackness. We know he hated Jesse Owens, or maybe just American blackness. We also know he hated all those who were claiming to be Jews. Regardless of whether everyone in Germany was claiming to be Jews or not, God does not enjoy it when emperors, dictators, pharaohs or kings decided whether his people should live or die.

In the western world, the universal sovereign rule of God's purpose is the most important relationship with man and God. Adolph Hitler and some of the new world age leaders, however, felt in their minds and their hearts it was predestined for them to do without God, because their relationship to God was not based on faith, but rather power. Why would we talk about a dreadful event such as the destruction of millions of people under the rule and leadership of Adolph Hitler, with his allies and enemies primarily responsible for the death of millions of God's people in the First and Second World Wars? When we look at history of the Gregorian Calendar, we are really only talking about a period of less than five hundred years. It is vain and just plain stupid to believe man can determine important prophecy, salvation, peace, love and regeneration.

No religious group or organization, church and or religious leader, can give any dead person a new life. Oh, I know there have been movies and books about men brought back from the dead, such men brought back from the dead, such as Dr. Frankenstein and other foolishness! We know that the Lamb, the TEMPLE, the house, the last prophet, and the great son of God, Jesus Christ, Lord and Savior, is the only one who raised people from the dead. In addition, He with the spirit and the Word of God – rose from the dead also. Much has been made about peace, and about being born again. Murderers have come out of prison, and while they were in prison someone told them if you just call on the name of Jesus you will be saved.

As a believer, not as a western world or an American Christian, neither as a good Jew or a black Hebrew Israelite believer, but as a believer of the Word of God and the spirit, I draw attention to the scripture where it is said: 'If a man, woman murder innocent blood send him or her to me.' We know that if we are in the flesh-and-blood terrestrial bodies, we are not in the presence of God, for it is written flesh and blood cannot inherit the kingdom of God. It is also written that to be absent from the body, flesh and blood is to be present before the Lord. Forgive us for what we are about to say. This is not commandment; we cannot speak for God, or even sit in the judgment seat of Jesus, the King of Kingsand Lord of Lords, and the great commander of God's heavenly band of ten thousand armies. We do know, however, that a murderer should be sent to God, and if we in the western world would just do what God has instructedus to do, maybe murderers would have the fear of God and respect for human life!

Isn't it strange that, in the western world, a murderer

will sometimes be the cream of the crop - the top of society – and almost always have money and is looked up to by his peers and associates? If the murderer is a poor person, these same peers of the rich man will throw the book at him! Hang him! Fry him! Gas the bastard! These are the kind of things that the peers of the rich men will say about the poor person. When it comes to judging the rich man, what do we hear from society? His peers will say, "Oh! I can't believe he or she did that! He has already paid for that, because everybody knows about him, plus he will have to face us at the country club, church or office. That's punishment enough. We feel so sorry for him, the murderer. Let's forgive him! We can identify with him and understandhis actions."

In the western world it is all or nothing. All if you are poor! Nothing if you are rich. Maybe, just maybe, that is why God said send them, the murderers, to him. While writing this book one of the very nice little ladies that was helping me asked a very thought provoking, questions. "Oh! So, you are for the death penalty?"

The question caught me off guard for a minute or so, and I did not, or could not, say "yes" or "no." Why then, are we even talking about a murderer in this book?

Who can answer these questions?

1. Did Cain kill or murdor Abol" If so, why?
2. Did Moses murder or kill an Egyptian leader?
3. Did Pharaoh kill or murder the Israelite people, or was murder in his heart (mind)?
4. Did David, the king of Israel or the babe, kill or murder the six-fingered and six-toed giant?
5. Did Rome or the Kenite Jews kill or murder Jesus Christ?

6. Did Hannibal kill or murder the people of the north side of the mountain Alps?
7. Did slave-traders kill or murder Africans in captivity, when moving them from their homeland to the utter most part of the world?
8. Did early settlers in America kill or murder the native American Indians? Or did the Indians kill or murder the settlers?
9. Did the Americans in the south kill or murder the American from the north, or was it the other way around" Did Yanks kill or murder the rebels?
10. Did Adolph Hitler and the German people kill or murder millions of people" Did millions of people kill or murder German people?
11. Did a nation or nations kill or murder PATRICE LUMUMBA? Or did Lumumba plan to kill or murder other nations?
12. Are nations killing or murdering people with AIDS, germ warfare, bombs, and bullets?
13. Why are we killing or murdering our babies? Is it just for money or is it for the love of money?

We will be the first to say, "God only knows!" All those questions were real easy compared to our next questions which are as follows:
1. Is a murderer more of a sinner than a born-again Christian who does not keep God's holy Sabbath?
2. Is a thieve more of a sinner than a liar?
3. Is a false witness more of a sin, than an adultereror the fornicator?
4. Which sinner does God love the most: the arrogant or the ignorant?

Any violation of sin is sin, only God knows. The most important question in all the contents in this book is this: Will you be ready for the regeneration of our Lord and Savior Jesus Christ? Or will you be caught up in the air? Satan, the devil, is the Lord and King of the air, nothingness, darkness, emptiness, hell. The Bible clearly states that of the first to be taken would be the first to go in the pit with Satan. Again, this salvation born again, saved with your own blood, speaking with you own tongue, roll over dipped in Crisco, baking soda and buttermilk Christianity; flying and lying, with your rapture doctrine that will lead you to an eternal damnation.

The writer of this book respects you and hopes you will ask yourself a particularly important question. Has everything that had been prophesied by the prophets of old (ancient Israelite prophets) and by our Lord and Savior Jesus Christ been fulfilled? "No!" I tell you these things: first, it is written in the twenty-fourth chapter of Matthew, the twelfth chapter of Mark twenty-sixth to the thirty-first verses, and in the book of Saint John and with the rest of the disciples of Jesus Christ; that in the end time, the first to come will be the antichrist or the Devil.

Our Lord and Savior has warned us that many will come in his name (Jesus Christ) claiming to be Christ, telling us Christ is here or there. Jesus warned us, believe them not, for many will come claiming to be Jews, Christians, born-again, for they do lie. As long as you are still breathing and when someone slaps you, and you still feel it, the end is not here yet. In the book of Daniel 7: 7-10:

> After this I saw in the night visions, and behold a fourth beast, dreadful and terrible, and strong exceedingly; and it had great iron teeth; it devoured and break in pieces,

and stamped the residue with the feet of it: and it was diverse from all the beasts that was before it; and it had ten horns.

I considered the horns, and, behold, there came up among them another little horn, before whom there were three of the first horns plucked up by the roots: and, behold, in this horn were eyes like the eyes of man, and a mouth speaking great things.

I beheld till the thrones were cast down, and the ancient of days did sit, whose garment was white as snow, and the hair of his head like the pure wool: his throne was like the fiery flame, and his wheels as burning fire.

A fiery stream issued and came forth from before him: thousand thousands ministered unto him, and ten thousand time ten thousands stood before him; the judgement was set, and the books were opened.

Before Jesus Christ left us, he warned us just as the prophet Daniel had spoken of the desolation of abomination. Then, after this momentous event, the destruction ofthe desolate, the dragon or Satan is judged by the Lord of Lords, King of Kings. In the final time before the real millennium, the devil and all those nations that have gone a- whoring and have been married to Satan, the antichrist, bybeing ministers of lies and deceit, and leading all nations tothe pit with their falsehoods and sin. Daniel completes this time of judgement in the very next verses: 11-13.

I beheld then because of the voice of the great words which the horn spake: I beheld even till the beast was slain, and his body destroyed, and given to the burning flame. As concerning the rest of the beasts, they had their dominion taken away: yet their lives were prolonged for a season and time. I saw in the night visions, and behold, one like the son of man came with the clouds of heaven and came to the ancient of days, and they brought him near before him. And there was given him dominion, and glory, and a kingdom, that all people, nations, and languages, should serve him: his dominion is an everlasting dominion, which shall not pass away, and his kingdom that which shall not be destroyed.

Make no mistake, my friends, my dear brothers and sisters, and all those who would declare themselves my enemies, this revelation and this prophecy is confirmed by Jesus Christ, who quoted Daniel and the desolation of abomination. Jesus made an astounding similar revelation through John, the last discipline of Jesus Christ. In the twentieth chapter of Revelation verses, 1-5, it states:

And I saw an angel come down from heaven, having the key of the bottomless pit and a great chain in his hand.

And he laid hold on the dragon, that old serpent, which is the Devil, and Satan, and bound him a thousand years,

And cast him into the bottomless pit, and shut him up, and set a seal upon him, that he should deceive the nations no more, till the thousand years should be fulfilled: and after that he must be loosed for a season.

And I saw thrones, and they sat upon them, and judgement was given unto them: and I saw the souls of them that were beheaded for the witness of Jesus, and for the Word of God, and which had not worshipped the beast, neither his image, neither had received his mark upon their foreheads, or in their hands; and they lived and reigned with Christ a thousand years.

But the rest of the dead lived not again until the thousand years were finished. This is the first resurrection.

My dear brothers and beautiful sisters, this is the only true millennium. Make no mistake: no man knows the time when this will take place, except Almighty God Jehovah. We do know that the prophecy in Ezekiel – thirty-seven through the forty-fourth chapter – has not taken place. We know as well that the great writer Paul warned us in I Corinthians 15: 50-58:

Now this I say, brethren, that flesh and blood cannot inherit the kingdom of God; neither doth corruption inherit incorruption.

Behold, I shew you a mystery; we shall not all sleep, but we shall all be changed,

In a moment, in the twinkling of an eye, at the last trump: for the trumpet shall sound, and the dead shall be raised incorruptible and we shall be changed,

For this corruptible shall have put on incorruption, and this mortal shall have put on immortality,

So when this corruptible shall have put on incorruption, and this mortal shall have put on immortality, then shall be brought to pass the saying that is written, Death is swallowed up in victory.

O death, where is thy sting? O grave, where is thy victory?

The sting of death is sin: and the strength of sin is the law.

But thanks to God, which giveth us the victory through our Lord Jesus Christ.

Therefore, my beloved brethren, be ye steadfast, unmovable, always abounding in the work of the Lord, forasmuch as ye know that your labour is not in vain in the Lord.

We pray that you study all the texts in the Word of God. However, we pray that you read the seventh chapter of Revelation, the forty-ninth chapter of Jeremiah, and learn about the four winds and the angels of the Lord who are still under the control of the Almighty God. We know that Jesus warned us that, although no man knows the time or the season, there are signs that help us be alert, waiting and watching for the true second coming of Jesus Christ. Be careful, my brothers and sisters, for as Jesus warned us, we may be under the sign of the fig leaf. Those of us whom God has chosen will understand this parable. As a friend, I want you to read the second and third chapter of Revelation, where we are warned by the Lord. Third chapter of Revelation 3: 6-11 verses reveals:

He that hath an ear, let him hear what the Spirit saith unto the churches.

And to the angel of the church in Philadelphia write; These things saith he that is holy, he that is true, he that hath the key of David, he that opened, and no man shutteth; and shutteth, and no man openeth;

I know thy works: behold, I have set before thee an

open door, and no man can shut it: for thou hast a little strength, and hast kept my word, and hast not denied my name.

Behold, I will make them of the synagogue of Satan, which say they are Jews, and are not, but do lie; behold, I will make them to come and worship before thy feet, and to know that I have loved thee.

Because thou hast kept the word of my patience, I also will keep thee from the hour of temptation, which shall come upon all the world, to try them that dwell upon the earth.

Behold, I come quickly: hold that fast which thou hast, that no man takes thy crown.

In the parable of the fig leaf we want to speak openly; we will not beat around the bush, for if we are God's chosen people, we would not deny Jesus Christ! We would not allow our government or our nations to pass laws and regulations that make it a criminal offense to speak the name of Jesus in our land.

Pharaoh made it a criminal act to just say the name 'Moses.' Not only was it a crime to say Moses, but the name Moses was stricken and removed from all the history books and literature in Egypt. Speaking as a young man who is now a mature person, I remember a history so terribly similar in America's Mississippi. In the whole south during the adoption of the 1890 constitution, an oppressed people could not say anything about freedom or their rights. They had limitations on what they could do, but the most incredible thing was that the old Mississippi plan, which was established when Reconstruction ended, not only forbade descendants of slaves to do and say certain things, but it was a crime for descendent of slaves and blacks to THINK they were equal or free. Does any of this have anythingto do with the rapture, SIN, or the regeneration of Jesus Christ?

We say to you, my brothers and sisters, that everything that is, and everyone who has ever lived will one day come before the throne of God. Then, the true millennium, that true one day of God, will become that true one- thousand-year millennium. Don't worry. It is going to be all right, because there is going to be a great getting upmorning. We all will be changed, Paul warned us, not so much when that time is, but how fast it is going to happen. When Satan and his false prophets are cast into the bottomless pit and chained, then that great prophecy written by Solomon, Daniel and all the major and minor prophets will come true, where it is written that one day to God is a thousand years for man.

SEE YOU AT THE REGENERATION!!!

I am the Lord thy God ...drawing by Van Leeuwen 1876
Courtesy of the Library of Congress

Egypt. Luxor. Statue of Rameses II in the Temple of Luxor.
Matson Photo Service. Courtesy of the Library of Congress

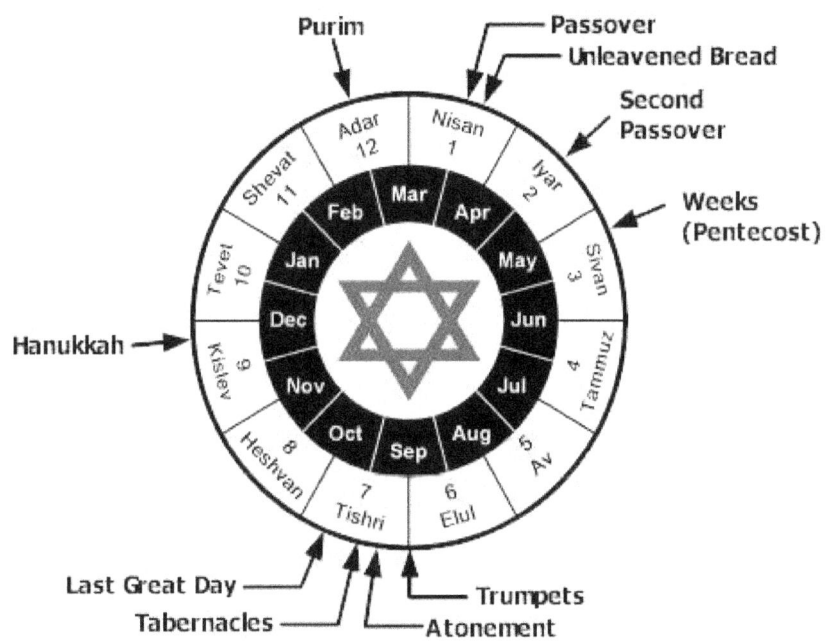

Hebrew Calendar

ABOUT THE AUTHOR

Robert Joseph Coleman, a native of Gadsden, Alabama, born April 10, 1939, was formerly an ice boy, a football star, a gourmet chef, a band member, a Marine, a business proprietor, a community activist, and a minister. He graduated from George Washington Carver High School in Gadsden, Alabama in 1957. He holds a Bachelor of Science degree in Biology from Jackson State College. He played a key role in the war against poverty in the Mississippi Cooperative Movement in the 1970s. He was also a political strategist and a trailblazer who ran for congress against incumbent Thad Cochran in 1976.

Make comments on the author's book page @
https://meredithetc.com/taata-time-and-after-time-ahead/

www.ingramcontent.com/pod-product-compliance
Lightning Source LLC
Chambersburg PA
CBHW071715140626
46557CB00011B/709